3

Shin Araki

Ilustration by
Maruyuki Morisawa

CLASSROOM FOR HEROES

"This is so inappropriate!
It's disgraceful!
Just die already!"

Earnest ❀

Former "Empress" of the academy. A lot of her not-so-appealing quirks have been on display lately.

❀ **Sophie**

A chill, quiet girl who feels a special bond with Blade.

"Heh...
Basking
in all the
attention
isn't
so bad."

Deemo/Maria ❀

Daughter of the Overlord. Her other, clumsier personality comes forward when she braids her hair. Joined the academy after taking an interest in Blade.

"Man, I feel so rejuvenated! This thermae is awesome!"

Claire ❀
A bashful late bloomer. Can't handle mixed-gender bathing.

Blade ❀
Former Hero and current normal student digging his slow-paced school life.

❀ **Yessica**
An uninhibited girl who got used to mixed bathing faster than anyone else.

Cú ❀
A young dragon who can turn into a person. Adores Blade as her "honored Father."

Land Mine Potato
Explodes if stepped on.

Gatling Green Peas
Spits out cannonball-sized peas at high speed.

Greater Mandrake
A giant humanoid carrot that curses anyone who digs it up.

Emperor Cabbage
The ruler of all cabbages.

Strength/tastiness: **2.5** DRAGONS

Kassim ✿
The shallowest boy in Earnest's gang. Always leaps out ahead and gets in deep trouble.

Strength/tastiness: **0.25** DRAGONS

Boxing Corn
The king of all corn.

Strength/tastiness: **3.0** DRAGONS

Clay

The most serious-minded
boy in Earnest's gang. Tends
to lurk in the shadows.

Strength/tastiness: 0.25 DRAGONS

❀
CONTENTS

CLASSROOM FOR HEROES

3

Shin Araki

Illustration by
Haruyuki Morisawa

YEN
ON
New York

SHIN ARAKI

Translation by Kevin Gifford
Cover art by Haruyuki Morisawa

This book is a work of fiction. Names, characters, places, and incidents are the product of the author's imagination or are used fictitiously. Any resemblance to actual events, locales, or persons, living or dead, is coincidental.

EIYU KYOSHITSU © 2015 by Shin Araki
All rights reserved.
Illustration by Haruyuki Morisawa.
First published in Japan in 2015 by SHUEISHA, Inc. English translation rights arranged with SHUEISHA, Inc. through Tuttle-Mori Agency, Inc., Tokyo.

English translation © 2024 by Yen Press, LLC

Yen On
150 West 30th Street, 19th Floor
New York, NY 10001

Visit us at yenpress.com • facebook.com/yenpress • twitter.com/yenpress
yenpress.tumblr.com • instagram.com/yenpress

First Yen On Edition: November 2024
Edited by Yen On Editorial: Emma McClain
Designed by Yen Press Design: Eddy Mingki

Yen On is an imprint of Yen Press, LLC.
The Yen On name and logo are trademarks of Yen Press, LLC.

The publisher is not responsible for websites (or their content) that are not owned by the publisher.

Library of Congress Cataloging-in-Publication Data
Names: Araki, Shin, 1968– author. | Morisawa, Haruyuki, illustrator. | Gifford, Kevin, translator.
Title: Classroom for heroes / Shin Araki ; illustration by Haruyuki Morisawa ;
translation by Kevin Gifford.
Description: First Yen On edition. | New York, NY : Yen On, 2024–
Identifiers: LCCN 2023055524 | ISBN 9781975378684 (v. 1 ; trade paperback) |
ISBN 9781975378707 (v. 2 ; trade paperback) | ISBN 9781975378721 (v. 3 ; trade paperback) |
ISBN 9781975378745 (v. 4 ; trade paperback) | ISBN 9781975378769 (v. 5 ; trade paperback) |
ISBN 9781975378783 (v. 6 ; trade paperback)
Subjects: CYAC: Fantasy. | Schools—Fiction. | Heroes—Fiction. |
LCGFT: Fantasy fiction. | Light novels.
Classification: LCC PZ7.1.A7216 Cl 2024 | DDC [Fic]—dc23
LC record available at https://lccn.loc.gov/2023055524

ISBNs: 978-1-9753-7872-1 (paperback)
978-1-9753-7873-8 (ebook)

10 9 8 7 6 5 4 3 2 1

LSC-C

Printed in the United States of America

CLASSROOM FOR HEROES

Shin Araki
Illustration by
Haruyuki Morisawa

Chapter 1:
Springtime at Rosewood Academy

Episode 1: Thermae Rosewood

○ Scene I: The Usual Training

Things were peaceful as usual at Rosewood Academy, with the students taking part in their normal afternoon drills.

Loud clanging filled the air as Blade helped Earnest out with her sword skills, just as he always did. Being her combat partner was a slog at the best of times, and since nobody else wanted to do it, Blade had little choice but to step up.

"Hah! …Hah! Haaaah!!"

Earnest was experimenting with a new move she'd just come up with. She wasn't holding back, either, slashing away like she didn't care if she killed Blade. All it would take was one misstep—if it was anyone but Blade, there would have been several fatalities during that day's drill alone.

So the clanging continued, sword against sword, with Blade yawning now and again. Earnest rewarded each one with a particularly lethal thrust.

"No yawning!" she'd shout, clearly offended.

Because she kept interrupting his yawns, Blade wasn't able to get out any really big ones, leaving him somewhat unsatisfied. This was the first class after lunch, and he couldn't shake off his desire for a nap. If Earnest insisted on hanging out with him, couldn't she at least agree to a nice lie down on the lawn instead?

Just then, the earth began to shake. Blade stopped and looked in the direction of the sound.

"What?" Earnest asked, lowering her sword and following his gaze.

But then she swung the tip of her weapon forward, catching Blade by surprise. She truly showed no weakness or hesitation.

Blade unconsciously avoided her strike. Unlike Earnest, he was wide open with his guard fully down. But, well—if he couldn't do this much, he shouldn't be calling himself an ex-Hero.

"What is it?" Earnest asked.

Whatever it was, was taking place outside the Proving Ground. They were simply taking part in a regular class, so the magical barrier was set to minimum strength, and patches of blue sky were visible between the structure's columns. There, on the other side, they saw a white pillar.

"I wonder what that is." Blade squinted. "For a little while now I've been sensing a powerful source of spirit on the move... I think something's going on."

What is that white pillar rising up in the distance? It looks a bit like water, but...

"Spirit?" Earnest muttered, sounding exasperated as she looked at Blade. "What the heck? How can you tell anything from so far away?"

Oh. So your average person can't tell, huh? Yet another bit of common sense for Blade to absorb.

○ Scene II: The Hot Spring

"Wha... What *is* this...?"

Earnest was stunned.

Blade was next to her, looking straight up and laughing. "Ah-ha-ha-ha-ha! Wow! Wow! Wowww!"

Water—hot water—was gushing out from the ground. No one knew why, but the liquid was practically scalding and was producing a tremendous amount of steam. The water surged up toward the sky, then fell back to the earth, by which time it was at just the right temperature.

"This is a hot spring. I've seen them before in my travels." Sophie was as cool as ever, despite being drenched from head to toe.

"Oh. So you call this thing a 'hot spring'?" Blade asked.

"They are a common phenomenon in volcanic regions. The water is heated by the temperature underground, then shoots up spontaneously. It's a natural occurrence."

"This one's not natural, though. Seems it was purposely dug up."

Dione, they now noticed, was lying on the ground, breathing hard. And she wasn't alone—there were two or three others with her... *Wait, aren't those champions?*

"Ladies and gentlemen! Do you know what a thermae is?" said a thundering voice.

Then the king himself stepped into view through the pouring water. His clothes, hair, and beard were soon soaked, but his gait retained its trademark ease. The women accompanying him were getting drenched, too. Sirene's vestments, in particular, had become so wet they were now basically sheer.

"What are you doing?" Blade asked.

He'd suddenly found himself unable to see. Earnest was covering his face with her hands.

"Don't look," she said.

"Why not?"

"Because I said so. Sophie, Yessica—you handle Leonard and Kassim for me. Clay, be a good boy, all right? You can close your own eyes. That's right. What a gentleman!"

It seemed the girls had taken care of Leonard and the others as well.

"A thermae, you see, is a public bathhouse!" bellowed the king. "That's what we in this kingdom used to call them!"

Blade could only hear the king's voice. His vision was completely blocked.

"And so, I hereby proclaim the establishment of the brand-new Thermae Rosewood right here, on this very spot!"

"You didn't establish jack!" shouted Blade. "All you did was dig up a hot spring—nothing's been built!"

"Right. My subjects, I leave the rest to you!"

Blade finally managed a peek through the gaps between Earnest's fingers. He could see a group of workers wearing helmets and matching jumpsuits trotting onto the scene, construction tools in their hands. This group of artisans was the same one that had helped convert the Proving Ground into a virtual-reality training facility.

"All right, folks!!" shouted the king. "The grand opening is in three days! Get ready for a watery paradise!!"

Blade and the other students walked away, the king's voice still ringing in their ears.

Oh, great. Here we go again.

○ Scene III: Thermae Rosewood

Hot water spurted endlessly out of a stone lion's mouth, pouring into a vast pool that stretched as far as the eye could see in all directions. The air was so thick with steam, it was impossible to make out the water's edge.

Blade and the other students were in the middle of an enormous open-air bath.

It really *had* taken only three days to complete Thermae Rosewood, the hot springs now installed as an addition to the academy's dormitory. It had been clear from their work on the Proving Ground that the men on the construction crew were no amateurs, and the speed and precision of their work on this latest project was further proof of their skill.

Incidentally, this hot spring had been dug out from a depth of over three thousand feet belowground. Apparently, if one dug that deep into the earth, hot springs could be found all over the place, not just in volcanic areas. Three champion-level fighters with skills suited to drilling had been summoned from across the kingdom specifically for this purpose— essentially just to dig a hole. According to the academy's doctor, they'd been so exhausted they wouldn't regain consciousness for the next two weeks. Blade hoped they were paid well, at least.

"Um, is anyone there?" A voice could be heard through the steam. Someone was approaching. "Oh, it's just you, Blade."

Leonard emerged from the haze. Blade could faintly hear him click his tongue in disappointment.

"Are you looking for someone?" Blade asked.

"Mmm? Well…kind of," he replied hesitantly. "I'm looking for girls…"

Immediately realizing who Leonard must be looking for, Blade said, "If you want Earnest, I don't think she's here."

"Oh, no, I didn't mean milady, I— Well, it's probably lucky for me that she's not around…"

He brushed his long wet hair away from his face, trying to look as cool as possible. But it didn't work on Blade. Most women would squeal at this act, but as a man, Blade wasn't moved at all by the gesture.

"Lucky how?"

"Well, *you* know…don't you?"

He didn't. But he did have a vague idea, at least, that Leonard had a thing for Earnest. Blade didn't quite understand what "having a thing" meant, really. If it meant loving someone, well, Blade loved everybody. This was probably a different kind of love, though. That was about all Blade could tell you. Blade also understood, more or less, that if Leonard "loved" Earnest, he'd probably find it thrilling to see her naked. But did Leonard want to get that thrill from *other* naked girls, too?

It didn't make sense to Blade… Would *any* girl work for him?

"But…boy, you gotta hand it to His Majesty, huh?" Leonard said, changing the subject.

"How so?"

"I mean…making this bath mixed gender. *Mixed gender!*" Leonard said those last two words in a hushed tone for some reason.

The king, who had designed this open-air bath, had apparently made that one of the rules. Since the space was mixed gender, the baths weren't divided into male and female sections.

Blade didn't understand why baths needed to be divided by gender in the first place. *Why can't everyone be together?* he thought. *Wouldn't that be more fun?* That way, he could be with all his friends at once. With separate baths, you could only be with one group of friends at a time. He had gone into the women's bath with Dione and the gang a little while ago, but then he'd been surrounded by girls, with none of the boys in sight. That was just as bad as being stuck on the boys' side. It'd be much more fun with everyone together, he thought.

"Hello!"

Yessica appeared out of the steam, waving her hands as she walked toward them. The hot water was splashing around the middle of her thighs. Blade followed Leonard's gaze upward from her thighs. *He's not looking at her boobs this time. Huh. Hmm. Hnnn?*

"Y-Yessica… don't *do* that… L-Leonard's here, too…!"

Claire was hunched over behind the bold and proud Yessica, looking as small as she could and clutching at the towel covering her body. Blade didn't understand why she felt the need to hide.

"Claire, are you implying that it'd be okay if it were just Blade here?"

"W-well, Blade…doesn't look at girls like that… Like a perv!"

"Well, *that's* rude. I'll have you know that I, Leonard Infermilord, have *never* looked lewdly at a woman's naked body. Not even once."

His gaze remained fixed on Yessica's lower half as he spoke. *Aha. So that's what Claire means by "like a perv."*

Blade tried to imitate Leonard's gaze. Kassim and Clay sometimes looked at girls like that, too, and as an aspiring "normal boy," Blade wanted to master the technique.

"Look!" Claire exclaimed. "Now Blade's copying him! Ugh! I *hate* you, Leonard!"

Oh wow, looks like Claire's gonna beat Leonard to death.

Leaving the three of them behind, Blade walked off, sloshing his way through the steamy water. It was time, he thought, to look for someone else. The first person he ran across was Sophie.

"Hey, there. Have you seen the king?" he asked.

Sophie pointed, and Blade changed course to head in the direction she'd indicated.

The gigantic outdoor bath was so big you could literally get lost in it.

But man… So Sophie's hair is blue down below, too. Blade turned around

to take another good look, but Sophie's small rear end had already disappeared into the steam.

o Scene IV: The King

The king had situated himself atop a large boulder, in what Blade assumed was the center of the outdoor bath.

"Oh, it's *you*, Blade!" he said, his robust figure sprawled out on the smooth stone. There were over ten beautiful women with him, lying around however they pleased, their well-developed nude bodies resting on the rocks and in the water.

"What do you think?" asked the king. "Are you enjoying yourself?"

"Mmm, I guess so," replied Blade. This big bath *did* feel pretty good, although he thought it might be a little *too* big.

"I had the water's mineral components analyzed," the king continued, "and let me tell you, this stuff's great for all *kinds* of things. They told me it helps with open wounds, nerve pain, muscle soreness, joint pain, shoulder tightness, motor paralysis, stiff joints, bruises, sprains, chronic digestive illness, hemorrhoids, cold sensitivity... The list goes on and on! It's supposed to be particularly helpful for convalescence and the promotion of good health. The perfect thing for you, don't you think?"

"I don't see what hemorrhoids have to do with me."

"As your king and ruler, I hereby command you to bathe here once a day."

"On what basis are you ordering me to do that?"

"All right, fine, I'll have the doctor prescribe daily visits to you later. *Then* will you do as I say?"

"Well, sure, but..."

Blade intended to come here every day whether he was ordered to or not. Normal people bathed once a day, after all. Blade knew that, and now that he was a normal person, he needed to take daily baths, too.

"Heh-heh-heh! I know how you feel. You can't get enough of this place, can you? A mixed-gender bath... Hee-hee! Pretty nice, isn't it?"

The king's mouth twisted into a smirk. Blade certainly wasn't complaining, since the mixed-gender rule let him bathe with his male and female friends at the same time.

"Leonard seemed pretty excited about it," said Blade.

"Oh? He's a man with potential, then. I wholeheartedly agree. It's truly wonderful to enjoy a soak while gazing at all these nubile young female bodies— Ow, ow! That hurts, Sirene."

The king was interrupted midsentence by Sirene giving him a painful-looking pinch.

"Why make the baths mixed gender, though?" Blade asked. The king was the one who came up with the idea, so Blade thought it best to take his question to the source.

"Because, you see, that is the law of our nation," the king said proudly. "It's written in the constitution, even. 'Every open-air bath must be fully accessible to both genders,' and so forth."

"That clause," Sirene noted pointedly, "was only added to the constitution three days ago."

A slender woman giggled at their exchange—the kingdom's minister of justice, if Blade remembered correctly.

The ladies surrounding the king were generally in positions of great authority, most of them ministers. But only in this corner of the mixed bath did they form what the general public would call a "harem" for the king.

Incidentally, a harem was a group of several women together with a single man. This was common sense, so of course Blade was familiar with it. As he was a completely normal person, it was natural for him to possess such knowledge.

"Well, have fun up there," Blade said as he turned around.

He waved as he walked through the water.

It was pretty hard finding his friends in this humongous bath. It was so big, it felt like once you got separated from someone, you might never see them again in your life.

Blade walked around at random, continuing his search.

○ Scene V: The Usual Dining Hall

Sometime later, Blade found himself in the usual dining hall, at the usual lunch hour. And as usual, it was a boisterous scene. The people sitting at his table—"Earnest's Gang"—were enjoying themselves, eating and chatting away.

"Hey," said Yessica, "how about we hit the bath after we're done eating?"

"What? But we don't have time," Claire replied. Yessica meant the open-air bath, of course—Thermae Rosewood.

"But we worked up a sweat during morning training, didn't we? I don't wanna be all sticky during the afternoon lectures."

"I know, but..."

Claire didn't seem too eager to adopt Yessica's proposal.

Blade was eating katsu curry for lunch as he always did, casually listening to everyone's conversations. Cú sat on his lap, and whenever she opened her mouth and said, "Ahhh," he would choose a piece of pork cutlet and thrust it into her mouth. He felt this was his duty as her honored Father. If there was any curry on what he fed her, the spiciness would make Cú breathe fire later on (literally), so he'd occasionally have to lick it off beforehand.

"You guys coming, too?" asked Yessica.

"Whoa... Wait a second, Yessica!"

For some reason, Yessica inviting the boys along was really distressing Claire. *I wonder why*, thought Blade.

"N-no... Ummm... I appreciate the invite, b-but..."

"Y-yeah... Uh, I think I'll pass, too..."

Clay and Kassim were similarly reluctant. They were both half standing up from their seats, ready to flee at a moment's notice. *Why?*

"Aww, too bad! ♡ How about you, Blade?"

"Mmm? Sure. What about you, Cú?"

The girl on his lap looked up at him and said in an adorable voice, "Race you to the other side, honored Father!"

"No!" a stern voice rang out.

It belonged to Earnest. She swirled her pasta around the tines of her fork, grimacing like she'd just bit down on something bitter.

"This mixed-gender bath has got to go. I-i-it... It's disgraceful!"

"But it's in the constitution," Blade shot back.

"Th-the king just wrote that in on a whim!"

"Shouldn't you call him 'His Majesty'? Aren't you being disrespectful?" Blade couldn't stop himself. After all, he was constantly being raked over the coals by Earnest whenever *he* did it. "And have you *still* not gone in yet?"

"Of *course* not!" Earnest shouted back.

"Yeah, but you need to bathe, don't you? You'll be all dirty otherwise."

"I *do* bathe! In my *dorm room*!"

Oh, right. Just like Blade's room, Earnest's was equipped with its own private bath. He'd found it pretty convenient at first, but now that he'd experienced the thermae, he didn't want to use that dinky little bathtub ever again.

"Don't you think she should try it, Cú?"

"I do indeed, honored Father."

Earnest could do little more than pout at Blade as he and Cú nodded at each other.

o Scene VI: The Thermae After School

Once afternoon classes were over, everyone marched right over to the thermae. They'd enjoyed a quick soak after lunch as well to get the sweat off their bodies, but this after-school bath was a wholly different beast. Now they had plenty of time to take a relaxing soak before dinner began.

"Honored Father! Watch me, watch me!"

Cú was dog-paddling around. It was Blade's job as her honored Father to respond by raising his hands above the water and waving back at her.

Beyond Cú, off in the distance, two large columns of water rose up.

Ein and Zwei, the twin spirit birds who became Blade's "children" after the most recent ruckus, were also in the bath. In fact, they had just plunged into the water headfirst from up above.

"Sure wish Earnest would come, too," Blade said to the person on his left.

"Right?" Yessica nodded.

"Don't you agree?" said Blade, this time addressing the person on his right.

"Certainly." Sophie nodded, too.

"Yessica… I respect you so much…," said Claire. For some reason, she was hiding behind a rock a little ways from the group. She always stayed nearby, yet she refused to come within five yards of them.

"Oh… Hey! Clay! Kassiiim!"

Blade spotted the two boys through the steam and waved at them. But for whatever reason, they offered only reserved waves and hesitant grins. *What was that supposed to mean?* It looked like they were trying to say, "No way, man."

"Hello, beautiful ladies!" cried Leonard. "What a coincidence that we should encounter each other here. May I join you?"

"Sure," Sophie said.

Yessica, however, crossed her arms and stared at Leonard. "There's no coincidence about it. You were making a beeline for us… It's only you, isn't it, Leonard? Why do all the other guys in school act like *that*?"

"Heh… Maybe they don't have a *bleeeep*."

"What's a 'bleep'?" asked Blade.

"Or maybe they're just really ashamed of their *bleeeep*."

"Again, what's 'bleep' mean?"

Something about Leonard and Yessica's conversation wasn't quite adding up.

"Nooooo! Ow, ow! *Stop* it! Ahhhhhh!"

Just then, someone screamed. Maria was walking toward them at a brisk pace.

"No! Deemo, nooooooo!" she shouted.

She might've been screaming her head off, but there wasn't a hint of hesitation in her gait. First her left braid came undone, then her right. And once her hair was free and running down her back…an arrogant expression appeared on her face.

Maria had what you might call a dual personality. When she undid her braids and let her hair down, she became the Overlord's daughter. The girls had nicknamed her "Deemo," a reference to her demonic origins, but the boys affectionately called her "Ovie" instead, taking inspiration from the word *Overlord*.

"Heh. What proud demon would ever hesitate to display her noble form?"

Ovie sat down on a large boulder nearby and elegantly crossed her legs. Sensing Leonard's gaze, she smiled thinly, then crossed her legs the other way.

As she lay on the wet rock, her breasts—between Sophie's and Yessica's in size—spread out a bit more than when she was standing, flattening out a little. *Wow. So breasts can move around like that? Funny.*

"Hee-hee… Like what you see?"

Sensing Blade staring at her, the girl cast him a bewitching look. *Huh? What does she mean?*

"It seems," she said, gazing into the distance, "that Blade is enamored with my nude form. I was fine with being his mistress, but it seems he's taken *you* instead."

Blade turned in the direction Ovie was looking and saw a red figure quickly duck behind a boulder.

"What're you doing, Earnest?" he asked.

"What? No! I'm not Earnest! You have the wrong person!"

"Is this a game? You gotta tell me the rules."

Earnest peeked out from behind the rock, exposing only the top half of her face.

"Give me a break!" she shouted. "He's with Sophie and Yessica…sandwiched between two pretty girls! I can't believe it! I can't *believe* it! This is so inappropriate! It's disgraceful! J-just die already!"

"Hey…Earnest? I can hear all that…"

"Ugh! All right! I'll come out!"

Earnest finally gave up and stepped out from behind the rock. She was covering her body with both arms, but she didn't really need to, since she was wearing a swimsuit. It was the same bright red bikini she'd worn while teaching Blade how to swim.

"Hey... Earnest, you're supposed to take off your clothes before getting in the bath."

"These aren't clothes, keh?! It's a bikini, keh?!"

"A bikini still counts as clothes." Blade sighed. "I heard that it's written into the constitution that 'bathers may not bring clothing or towels into public baths.'"

The document went on to specify that swimsuits counted as clothing. It was as if the framers had foreseen attempts to skirt the rules and nipped them in the bud.

"Hey, Anna...? Why not just give up already?" said Yessica, now one of Earnest's best friends. "Besides, you've already exposed yourself plenty of times."

"I have done no such thing..."

Every time Earnest transformed into the Scion of Flame, whatever she was wearing at the time was burned to ashes. She couldn't stay in Scion mode for very long, thanks to how many calories it consumed, and whenever she turned back, she'd wind up in her birthday suit. The sight of her running around like that carrying her sword had earned her the rather unsavory nickname the "Nude Avenger."

"Yeah, you have," Yessica replied. "With all the time you spend running around naked, what's the point of getting embarrassed now? It makes no sense." And this was one of her *best friends* speaking, mind you.

"Well... I mean, that was during *battle*, keh?! I didn't have a choice, keh?!"

Earnest had a point. You couldn't survive in battle if you were preoccupied with how much you were wearing.

"Exactly!" someone called out. "You can't afford to be picky in battle!"

It seemed they agreed with her.

○ Scene VII: Earnest's Trial

The speaker strode up to them, splashing water as he walked and shouting in his throaty voice. It was none other than His Majesty, the king.

"Y-Your Majesty!"

Earnest fell to one knee, greeting her monarch. Everyone took various measures to appear more dignified. Everyone, that is, except for Blade; Sophie, next to him; Ovie, still splayed out atop her rock; and Cú, swimming off in the distance.

"But you must understand!" he shouted, standing tall with his arms folded in front of him. "This bath is just another type of practical training!"

"Your Majesty! Your—your front! Can you hide your front, please?! That thing's like a deadly weapon." Yessica had her hands over her eyes, but she was nevertheless staring right at the king through the wide-open gaps between her fingers.

"On the front lines, there is no time to change, no time to shower, and no separate facilities for men and women! In *my* kingdom's military, all changing rooms are mixed gender!"

"But why?!" shouted Earnest.

Shockingly, she was lashing out at the king. She was always getting on Blade's case for being rude to the monarch, and yet here she was, doing the same thing.

"Forgetting about the constitution for a moment," said Blade, "he's right about the front lines, you know. It's like that for everyone."

He wasn't all that interested in defending the king…but on this point the man was right, so Blade felt obliged to say something to Earnest.

"What?!" she exclaimed. "Why?!"

"Well, I mean… It's always been that way."

For Blade, who'd been born and raised on the battlefield, it seemed much weirder to have separate facilities for men and women. There were no men or women on the front lines—everyone was a person, a soldier, first. Soldiers didn't go around shrieking like women or howling like men when they chopped someone in half. Why would such people waste their limited resources building a second set of facilities when only one was needed? In battle, winning was the supreme objective—comfort and privacy were of no importance. Any feelings of shame or discretion had to be thrown out the window.

"That's how it is," said the king. "So, Earnest, please disrobe."

"What is that supposed to mean?!" Earnest exclaimed.

"It means exactly what I said. This is practical training."

"But…!"

"Earnest, you're the academy's top student, right?"

"Huh? Well…yes…" For some reason, she looked back at Blade before nodding to the king.

"If you don't step up and lead by example, what are the rest of the students to do?"

"Huh? Even this…?!"

"Enough of your whining! I don't want to hear it! I don't want to hear it!" The king stamped his feet like a child. "All I want…is to look…at naked young girls! I want to, I want to, I *want* to!"

He began stamping more excitedly. He was acting like a real brat. And whenever he stamped his feet, the thing in between his legs bobbed around, too. The girls all called it a "deadly weapon," and before long, it had progressed from simply bobbing and was spinning around like a propellor. Clockwise.

"Look out, Earnest!" Blade shouted irresponsibly. "I think he's testing your loyalty!"

"…Very well," Earnest said, her voice fierce and grand, as if reverberating from deep below the ground. "But…I have an idea of my own."

It was unclear what Earnest's "idea" was, but she whipped out the sword she'd been holding behind her back and lunged for the king. The tip was pointed straight at him and never wavered. The monarch, exposed in a number of ways, froze up. His "deadly weapon" stopped spinning and drooped toward the ground.

Did Earnest seriously bring her sword into the bath? That's gotta be even worse than wearing clothes. Though I guess the constitution didn't say anything about swords…

"Look out, King!" Blade shouted casually, "I think she's testing your right to rule!"

Why is the old man so scared of a sword? Didn't he go through a whole lot worse back in the day?

"Earnest, please, calm down," said the king.

"I will not. Based on your words, I have made my decision. I ask your permission to use my sword."

"Whoa, whoa, I can't permit that. I really can't. If you insist, we could reconvene later and use VR. Yes, let's go with that."

"No, Your Majesty. I wish to carry out your order at once. 'No one is allowed to use the thermae while wearing clothes,' correct?" Earnest's voice was calm and composed.

"Whoa, whoa, whoa. Um… Let's leave that sort of thing to Sirene alone, all right?"

Blade wasn't quite following. What did the king mean by "that sort of thing"? Earnest might've had her sword out, but Blade wasn't worried. He knew she had no intention to kill the king. He couldn't sense any bloodlust from her.

Earnest readied her sword, raising it high above her head… And then it ignited.

Asmodeus was engulfed in white-hot flame, which spread from the sword's grip to Earnest's arms, and then to her entire body. Soon, she had transformed into a giant column of fire. Hot air blew out from her vicinity, evaporating some of the water into steam.

Once the steam cleared, they could see the Scion of Flame before them. The charred remains of Earnest's red bikini were floating in the water.

"*Well? I'm naked now, aren't I?*" she said.

Her voice came from the vicinity of what would have been her face, but its strange tone seemed to emerge from the vibrations of the air itself. Being pure flame, her head was constantly changing shape, making it hard to gauge her expression… But she was probably flashing them a smug smile as usual. Actually, Blade was sure of it. He didn't even have to look.

"Hey, Earnest?" he said.

"*What?*"

The Scion of Flame put her weight on one leg and brought a hand to her hip—the classic "I'm better than you" pose.

"That's not really fair, is it?"

"*Not fair? What's not fair? Why not? …You're kidding, right? You all told me to get naked, so I did. See? I'm totally nude! I'm not wearing anything at all! Does anyone have any complaints? They don't, do they?*"

Blade shrugged, then turned to face the others to ask their opinions, when—

"*Boooooooooooooooooo!!*"

A loud chorus of boos broke out.

"*Hey! What's the problem? What's wrong with this?! All the constitution says is that clothing is prohibited in the thermae! It doesn't say anything about transforming! Does it? Does it?!*"

"*Booooooooooooooooooooooooooooooooooooo!!*"

The booing showed no signs of stopping. It was growing louder and louder into a mighty chorus of sound.

"Hey, Earnest?" Blade said. "There's a weird sound coming from your feet."

Earnest had transformed into a pillar of fire, a highly dense mass of flame in the shape of a human… So naturally, when she was submerged in water, it began to boil. Sizzling sounds erupted from below her.

"Hey, Earnest! Over here! It's getting a little chilly!"

Blade beckoned Earnest over. He liked the wide-open feel of the bath, but he preferred the water to be just a tad warmer.

"Anna! Over here, too!"

"And here as well, milady!"

"Come here for a second, Earnest." Even the king wanted some.

Earnest was now the life of the party, serving as the bath's heating unit.

"*Do I look like a pile of kindling or something?!*" she shouted—but there was no arguing that she was a viable heat source. "*Ugh! Okay! Who's first?!*"

And so Earnest did the rounds, heating one spot, then the other, sending up bubbles, and generally firing up the bathscape. Then, after a while…

"Oh no… Wait… Ah, I'm fading out… Why so fast?"

Transforming into flame ate up a lot of calories—one million per hour, just to stay lit. Four days' worth of calories were consumed in just one minute, and even at her most rotund, Earnest couldn't last longer than half an hour. Now that she was in good shape, she fizzled out a lot quicker.

"Well, evaporating all this water is probably gobbling up a few times more energy than usual, right?"

"I'm fading out… Fading out… No… If I fade out now…!"

Earnest writhed around, groaning and moaning. But it was all in vain. Her flames disappeared, and her body re-formed—naked, of course. Nothing beyond her birthday suit ever came back. Entering Scion mode burned away whatever she was wearing, including swimsuits.

"Don't look at me!" With a splash, Earnest crouched down in the water, covering her chest with both hands.

"Anna," said Yessica, sounding exasperated. "As I said, don't you run around like that all the time on the battlefield?"

"I'm always so impressed, Anna," said Claire, another of Earnest's best friends. "I could never run around like that in the middle of a fight."

Unbeknownst to Claire, this was the final straw. She was probably honestly impressed. But taken the wrong way, her words were like a sharpened knife to Earnest's heart.

Earnest, still crouching, shook a little. Her shoulders, visible above the water's surface, were quivering. Blade took this opportunity to say something neither of her two friends had.

"If you say not to look, I won't."

He had no idea why she didn't want people seeing her naked. But if she didn't want to be looked at, he wouldn't look.

"…Really?" Earnest asked, her shoulders no longer shaking.

"Have I ever lied to you?"

"Are you sure? You promise?"

"Yes, I promise."

"You swear you won't look? You swear?"

"Yes, I swear."

"Say it one more time. Promise me."

"Aw, you're like a little princess!" said Yessica.

Earnest glared at her, sending a shock wave across the water and causing it to splash all over. *See? Her glares are as good as punches!*

"If you say you don't want me to look, I won't look. Though if you want me to look, I can do that, too."

"Fat chance."

"Wow, Blade, that's so deep…"

Another shock wave ran through the water and exploded with a splash. Yessica somersaulted out of the way.

"C-could I…," Earnest began.

"Hmm? Could you what?"

Earnest was trying to say something, so Blade patiently waited for her to continue.

"Could I come over there?"

"Hmm? Sure. I don't mind."

Earnest tiptoed over to Blade, her back still turned to him. Then, from behind, she pressed up against him, skin to skin.

"I'm here," she said, her back against his.

"Yeah."

Oh, I see. If we put our backs together, neither of us can see the other naked. Earnest is so smart.

Blade looked up. The sun was setting, and the sky was dyed a gradient from orange to dark blue. The two moons, one larger than the other, were just starting to appear. Birds flew across the orange part of the sky, returning to their roosts as a cool breeze whistled through the air, clearing away the bath's steam.

"Hey… How about—?" Blade began, addressing Earnest.

"N-no. We can't! It's not proper!"

"What're you talking about?"

"Huh? Wait, what did you mean?"

"What a princess!" shouted Yessica.

Glare. Plish-plish-plish. Splash!

"I meant the bath," Blade said.

"Huh?"

"How about this bath, Earnest? Nice, isn't it?"

Blade was spending time with his friends under the open sky, in this giant hot spring. What could be better? *Nothing, that's what.*

Blade pushed up against Earnest's back, relaxing and leaning against her. She didn't object.

"Oh...? Um, hey—"

"It's nice, isn't it?" Blade said to a flustered Earnest.

Seconds passed, then minutes.

"...Yes," she said at last.

It wasn't clear whether she liked being leaned on or the bath in general, but either way, her answer was *yes*.

Episode 2: Love on the Boys' Side

○ Scene I: The Usual Training

"Hey, Blade, who do you think will win?"

"Good question. The winner, I guess."

It was a typical afternoon, and they were having their usual training.

Just as he always did, Blade was fielding Earnest's questions as he caught her strikes, their swords clanging. They were discussing the teams next to them. Clay, Kassim, Yessica, and Claire were all friends, but today they had divided into opposing pairs—the guys against the girls. Maybe that was why they were even louder than usual.

"Is that some kind of joke?" Earnest asked.

With a mighty swing, she launched a fireball. She hadn't even needed to charge.

"I didn't mean it as one."

The fireball was a good ten feet in diameter, but Blade slashed it in half.

He really *hadn't* meant it as a joke... So why had Earnest hit him with a fiery punch line hot enough to turn most people's bones to ash?

On the battlefield, there was no way to predict who would win. Even the most experienced veteran was one errant stab away from defeat. Unreliable buffoons who look like they'll never survive often wind up doing just that. In battle, the person who wins isn't necessarily the strongest— they're just the last person standing. *That* was what Blade meant.

Earnest came to a stop and began watching the contest unfolding next to them, leaving Blade with nothing to do.

But man...this sword is amazing. Blade looked down at the weapon in his hand. He had run a quick streak of fighting force through it, and it hadn't dulled at all. The sword, which he'd been supplied with recently, was actually a pretty decent article. It might even be comparable with a magic blade like Asmodeus. If he took good care of it, it should last him about a week or so.

Since Earnest was no longer interested in practicing, Blade sheathed his sword and went to stand next to her.

"Yessica!" "Claire!"

As for the girls, Yessica responded to their classmates' cheers with a wink and a "Hel-loooo! ♡" while Claire was too embarrassed to look up from the floor.

"Clay!" "Kassim!"

And as for the guys, Clay awkwardly stiffened up at the girls' high-pitched cheers, while Kassim rewarded his audience with a backflip.

As a handsome, serious-minded swordsman, Clay was popular with the girls at the academy. Kassim, a frivolous flirt, was popular, too, in his own way.

They, along with Claire and Yessica, had moved up from the junior class. Going from the junior class to the senior one was said to be quite difficult, and the four of them had achieved a measure of fame among the students. Other well-known students like Earnest, Leonard, and Sophie were in the senior class, too, but they'd been there since joining the academy, and the cheers were always louder for the former juniors.

These four were also the first friends Blade made while he was in the junior class. He was promoted in a matter of days, and they'd promised to join him. And true to their word, they'd become seniors less than a month later.

"Who are you rooting for, Blade? Claire, I bet."

Why Claire? And why was Earnest betting on it?

"I'm rooting for anyone," he said. "The strongest fighter's gonna win. That's all there is to it." This was the undeniable truth of the battlefield.

"Didn't you say 'Whoever wins is the strongest' earlier?"

"Yeah. That's true, too."

To be precise, whoever was left standing at the end—whoever survived—was the winner. Perhaps it was his nature as an ex-Hero, but Blade couldn't help unconsciously gauging his classmates' strength.

Despite the hopes of the cheering audience, there was a clear strength imbalance between the two teams. One side included Clay, an orthodox swordsman, and Kassim, an assassin. Meanwhile, the other was composed of Yessica, an aspiring spy whose focus wasn't on brute strength, and Claire, who was more like a medic with a violent streak. It was obvious which side had the advantage.

"Look," Earnest said. "It'll be over soon."

Blade focused in on the fight.

Claire's morning star bashed into Clay's head, sending his cranial fluids flying. They were doing VR training today, so this wasn't a problem. There was no reason to stop your weapon before it made contact in the virtual world. The dead were simply removed from the space, forced back to the real world alone to ruminate on what they did wrong.

"Huh? ...We won? Really?"

"Yaaaay!"

Claire and Yessica took each other's hands and began to hop around, flashing peace signs. Kassim, meanwhile, was on the ground in a pool of his own blood. The gore was censored for most of the class, but Blade, with his "Hero's-eyes-only" special cut, saw all of it in full detail.

"See?" said Blade. "You never know how it'll turn out."

"Guess not. Seems like you were right, Blade."

Earnest, too, had expected the men to win. But in the end, she'd been wrong. That was war, for you.

"...Attention!" she shouted in a loud, clear voice.

For a moment, she was the Empress. All it took was that single word to make everyone turn around and listen up.

"Okay, Blade," she said. "Explain for the class!"

"Huh? You want *me* to tell them?"

"Yes. And be quick."

Blade reluctantly turned to face the others.

"Well," he began, "the girls' team won because they diligently kept up their studies."

About half of the class had been watching the fight. For the other half, Blade gave a brief recap. He had been busy fighting Earnest and marveling at his sword, but his senses could pick up what was going on around him without requiring any visuals. He could perceive anything that happened within a fifty-yard radius in minute detail. He had to be capable of that much, or someone could blindside him from behind. Such skills were required of a Hero. Not that he was a Hero anymore, but still.

The biggest key to Yessica and Claire's victory just now was Claire's progress. These days, she was able to swing her morning star while cleverly taking advantage of her restoration ability. That allowed Yessica to pull all kinds of risky stunts without fearing death. This still took guts, the mental strength required to endure the pain, and full trust in her partner—but Yessica had all of those things. That was amazing in itself. She would jump into the fray, knowing she'd be sliced by her opponent's sword, get sliced for real and restored, then attack like a zombie. Even Blade would probably hesitate a little. He didn't like pain very much.

Recently, the First Proving Ground's VR setup had received an upgrade, allowing it to simulate Claire's restoration ability. Blade doubted the boys would ever be able to win at this rate.

"And as for why Clay and Kassim lost..." He debated whether or not to say what he was thinking for a moment, then gave in. "Well, they *weren't* being diligent. They were resting on their laurels strength-wise."

The two of them weren't there to hear any of Blade's comments. Clay had died from having his head smashed in, and Kassim had passed away from blood loss, so they were now back in the real world. Nevertheless, Blade was sure they'd find out through the grapevine. As hard as it was to say, he was blunt.

"They got too proud and neglected their training," he said, as clearly as he could, so the message would get back to them from their classmates.

After all, wasn't that what friends were for?

o Scene II: The Boys Reflect

Once the class bell rang and everyone returned to reality, Blade found Clay and Kassim scowling and wondering where they went wrong. They were sitting on the ground, right where they had gone down, their eyes fixed on a point a few dozen feet away as they mumbled and grumbled. Their fingers were so tightly clenched around their knees that their knuckles had turned white.

"Um... Clay? K-Kassim?" Claire tried to call out to them.

The boys were visibly shaken; they both turned toward the girls, a cold sweat breaking out on their faces.

"Y-you don't need to worry...about the fight," Claire continued. "I think that was just a fluke...probably."

"No, no... I was just thinking about it, and I think it's down to a lack of ability on our part..."

"No, it's not! I know you two are stronger than us, Clay."

Claire was probably trying to be nice, but her words only plunged the boys into even greater despair.

"Blade?" Earnest said.

"Yeah?"

"You know what they say about rubbing salt in people's wounds?"

"Huh, I've never heard that before, but sure."

"I think I finally understand exactly what they mean."

"Actually, me too." Blade nodded.

"Um... I'm sorry we won!" Claire placed her hands together and bowed, making her long black hair sweep forward. That proved to be the last straw.

"Ngh... *Waaaaaaaaaaaahh!*"

Clay and Kassim both ran away, crying. Kneeling on the hard ground must have made their legs fall asleep, because they tripped a few times before they managed to sprint out of sight.

"They were crying!"

"They sure were."

"Why would they cry?"

"Oh, great, you made them cry…"

"You really did it."

"What losers!"

Several of the girls gave their comments—Yessica, Earnest, Sophie, Maria, Ovie, and Cú, in that order. The others looked on with blank stares. Most of them appeared not to comprehend what was happening. The guys, on the other hand, were all sympathetic, including Blade.

Yep, I can see why they'd cry. Claire really laid it on thick…

○ Scene III: Meeting in the Bath

"Hey, cheer up already."

It was late at night, and Blade was relaxing in the outdoor bath with Clay, Kassim, and a few others—a meeting with everything out in the open, so to speak. Blade was trying to soothe the depressed boys' feelings, then cheer them up a bit.

The thermae was almost too spacious. If you sloshed your way far enough back into the water, there were plenty of isolated spots with no one else around.

I wonder if you'd call this a "boys' night"? Blade knew that Earnest sometimes held "girls' nights" where only women were invited. So if only guys were present, would it be correct to call this a boys' night? *…Yeah, probably.*

"All you did was lose once," he said. "Just try to win next time."

"You don't understand, Blade. Like, you've *never* lost to a girl, right? Or to anyone."

"No."

"See?" Clay said.

"But I wouldn't really care if I did."

He wasn't a Hero anymore, so why care if he lost? Back when he was a Hero, he couldn't afford to lose. If a Hero lost, it would mean the end of the human race.

"But I *do* care. I wouldn't mind losing to other people, but…losing to Yessica…"

"Why don't you want to lose to Yessica?" Blade asked.

He'd figured Clay was just being a sore loser, but it seemed this was more about a personal rivalry. Did he see Yessica as his rival? But why her?

"Oh, you know."

"No, I don't."

Clay let out a deep, heavy sigh. Then he looked Blade square in the face, as if he was about to make a monumental confession.

"I mean...you know... I—I—I...l-l-l-love... I mean, I l-love...I love Yessica!"

"Hmm."

"That's your response?!"

"Well, I love her, too."

"Huh? Whoa! Y-you *do*?! Well... That's kind of bad for me, isn't it?!" Clay looked panicked. *What's he worried about?*

"Blade! Hey, Blade..." Kassim poked Clay with his elbow, signaling that he'd take over. "I thought you were into Earnest or Sophie or Ovie or someone like that. Was I wrong?"

Clay eagerly nodded his head.

"Sure," Blade replied. "I love Earnest, and Sophie, and Ovie, too. I love everyone."

"Huuuh?! You *do*?!"

"And you too, Clay. And you, Kassim."

"What? Oh... Man, don't scare me like that. You meant *that* kind of love." Clay and Kassim now looked relieved. "That's not the kind we meant."

"How's it different?"

"You wouldn't understand," said Kassim as Clay nodded along. "You've never liked a girl, have you?"

"Hmm..." Blade pondered this, arms crossed. "Do you mean like, wanting to take a bite out of them?"

Long, long ago, when Blade was around five years old, he'd latched on to Dione's rear end. It had looked tasty to him, like a big slab of horse meat.

"Absolutely not," said Kassim.

"I see." Blade nodded. *Didn't think so.*

"H-hey," Clay interrupted, "Isn't that actually kinda close, though?"

"Hmm. Maybe you're right…" Now Kassim was wavering, too.

"Well, which is it?" asked Blade.

"A-anyway," replied Clay, dodging the question, "I love Yessica, all right?" He puffed out his chest.

"And, as I'm sure you've realized," Kassim said, joining in, "I like Claire—"

"I realized just now, yeah."

"Claire is just…so nice. Really pure and serious. Kind, too. Isn't she the best? Like, she's just so authentic. Maybe it'd be a waste for her to end up with a wild guy like me."

"Whoa, hold on a minute. What do you mean by 'authentic'? Are you saying there are inauthentic girls? And Kassim, you're more flirty than wild, and I think everyone else would agree."

"She's so beautiful as she bludgeons you to death. She's pretty merciless sometimes, too. But that's just another one of her charms."

"Listen to what I'm saying, will you?"

It was true that Claire was occasionally brutal, and she usually struck the final blow in a fight, as she'd done earlier against Clay and Kassim.

"But Yessica's amazing," said Clay. "She's such a free spirit—so uninhibited. But maybe she wouldn't be a good match for an uninteresting guy like me."

"A free spirit? What makes you say that?"

"L-like…how she has all that experience, you know?"

"Experience with what?"

"Especially since she was promoted to the senior class. I mean, just look at her outfit… You get it, right?"

"Listen to me."

"But despite all that, she's really compassionate. She might seem unprincipled at first, but she's actually a kind, sensible girl."

"I *said* listen to me."

Clay was a lost cause, too. The conversation wasn't going anywhere. But…Yessica, a free spirit? What was that supposed to mean?

"You mean like how they pop out?" he asked.

Come to think of it, they popped out on him not long ago. When it came to gravity, she truly *was* a free spirit.

"What popped out?" Clay asked, looking at him.

"Oh, so now you're listening."

"What is it? Tell me. Spill the beans. You're not allowed to keep secrets."

"Well, I joined her in the girls' bath the other day..."

"Way to bury the lead... So what happened?"

"Well, the top of her swimsuit slipped a little, and they kind of popped out."

"You saw them?!"

Clay seemed weirdly agitated by this. Blade wasn't sure why. Just because she had a pair of free spirits on her chest... What was the big deal?

"I dunno, it was more like she showed them to me. But you can see them here in the thermae whenever, right? You've seen them, too."

"I've never dared to look!"

"Do you want to see them or not?"

"I do, I do! But I can't! Don't you understand?!"

"I'm afraid I don't..."

Blade crossed his arms as he sat in the hot water, his face scrunched up in a frown.

This sounded like a deep, esoteric problem...

○ Scene IV: Cú the Adviser

"So that's what has you two down in the dumps? No problem! You just gotta get stronger!"

"Waaah!"

"Whoa!"

Clay and Kassim were so startled by the sudden sound of Cú's voice that they half leaped out of the water.

"When did *you* show up?!" asked Clay.

"I've been here awhile," she replied.

Cú had followed the boys to the thermae and started doggy-paddling a little ways away. *Did they really not notice her? They must both be pretty freaked out...*

"Oh, right," said Blade. "Cú, come here!"

"What is it, honored Father?"

"Look," he said, turning to the other boys. "Here are some boobs."

He hooked his arms under Cú's armpits and held her up in the air. He knew Clay and Kassim loved boobs popping out.

"No, man! I'm not talking about *those* kinds of breasts!"

"Well, I guess it's something..."

"Which is it?" Blade asked, confused.

"Honored Father? I feel like people are saying rude things about me."

"Those two have been acting weird for a while now. Just ignore them."

"Okay! I'm a generous girl! And I *am* a female, just so you know. If you want to know how girls feel about things, feel free to ask me."

"A-are you sure?"

"Maybe we should!"

The duo were convinced. Blade wasn't so sure, but he decided to play along with Cú.

"So Clay and Kassim are in love with Yessica and Claire," he explained.

"Yeah, I love them, too!" said Cú.

"Right, but apparently it's not *that* kind of love."

"Yes, I know. They love them as a male loves a female."

"Oh, you understand?"

Blade was still oblivious, but it seemed Cú knew what she was talking about. What an intelligent girl. Blade's chest swelled with pride.

"So you guys want to know how to make the girls you like love you back?" he said, confirming. The two other boys nodded, now sitting upright and paying full attention.

"Well, *that's* really easy," said Cú, pounding a fist against her meager breasts.

"It is?!"

"Th-then tell us!"

There was a desperate tone to Clay's and Kassim's voices as they shuffled closer to her, still kneeling.

"Females love strong males," Cú continued. "So just become stronger. Once you're strong, the females will be all over you. They'll melt in your arms!"

"Th-they will?" they replied. Then, nodding vigorously, they snapped their gazes to Blade for some reason.

Was that really how it worked? Blade had his doubts. But he didn't understand the subtleties of male-female relationships, and if Cú claimed she did, he figured she was probably right.

"B-but we're already pretty strong. How can we get even stronger...?"

"That's really easy, too!" Cú pounded her small breasts with her fist again for effect. "Just have my honored Father give you special training!"

"...Me?" Blade pointed at himself.

"Please!"

"Yes, I'm begging you!"

Faced with Clay's and Kassim's overwhelming enthusiasm, Blade had no choice but to acquiesce. The two of them were his friends, after all, and he'd do anything for a friend.

o Scene V: Girls' Night In

"All right," said Earnest, nodding to herself. "So you want to make up with Clay and Kassim?"

There was an arrangement of tea and snacks laid out on the table before her. She had a lot of tea, in fact—girls met up in her dorm room pretty often, so she kept a ready supply of the best tea leaves she could find. She had lots of snacks, too—an almost inexhaustible supply. Earnest was grabbing them by the handful, while Yessica and Claire enjoyed only a little at a time, plucking up bite-sized portions with their fingertips. Earnest could go on a flame diet whenever she needed to lose weight, but that wouldn't work for the others.

"The problem is that whenever we try talking to them, they run off," said Yessica.

"Yeah," agreed Claire. "Kassim won't even get within speaking range of me."

"Wow. That's so disgraceful," said Earnest. "I can't believe they're that bothered by one loss. I mean, really? Why are guys so soft?"

"I know." Yessica brought a hand to her cheek.

"...You think we should lose for them next time?" asked Claire.

"No, that'd be even worse," said Yessica. "That might knock them out forever."

"Oh, you think? So losing's no good, either?"

"Yep."

"Then what *should* we do?"

"That's simple!" someone said, reaching a thin arm between Yessica and Claire to grab as many snacks as they could hold.

"Whoa! You were here, Cú?"

"I sure was! Earnest's room is like a free snack buffet!"

"Try to hold back a *little*, all right?"

"Hey, Cú, how is it 'simple,' huh? What should we do?"

"Males love strong females. So just become stronger. Once you're strong, the males will be all over you. They'll melt in your arms!"

Yessica and Claire visibly winced.

"W-we don't really want them all over us..."

"Yeah...right? Neither of us are that kind of girl, are we?"

"Oh, you're not?" asked Earnest.

"What do you mean, Anna?"

"N-no...never mind. It's nothing."

"You're acting weird, Anna."

"Yessica...," said Claire. "How about we just go easy on the training for a while and let the boys overtake us?"

"No way!" said Earnest. "That'll never work!"

Claire immediately gave in. "No, I guess not..."

"Listen, you two. Are you both fine with things as they stand?"

"Well, no, but..."

"I want to do *something*."

Claire and Yessica both looked down at the floor.

"In that case," Earnest said with a wink. "It's not just Cú who has an idea."

○ Scene VI: The Rematch

The afternoon training session was over, but not a single person had left the old Proving Ground. Instead, the atmosphere was strangely charged.

Clay and Kassim, along with Yessica and Claire, were staging a duel to the death...or rather, comparing the results of their training. The fight would be decided according to the king's rules for practical training: Weapons and magic were allowed, as were unique special abilities, surprise attacks, and any other trickery. It would be very similar to real battle. Victory was achieved by killing one's opponent—a rule only feasible in the virtual world.

Everyone had whined about the VR training when it was first instituted. But by now they were more than accustomed to it and had stopped fussing over who died or didn't die, who killed someone or was killed, or who ate or didn't eat whom. They were on such a high level that even if they were thrown onto the front lines, they'd be able to hold their own with grizzled veterans. Blade hated to admit it, but the king seemed to know what he was doing.

"Clay!"

Cheers erupted. The studly swordsman was as popular as ever among the girls, though he only had eyes for Yessica.

"Yessica! Claire!"

The girls were popular, too, mostly among the female students. The boys probably liked them a lot, as well, but for some reason, none of them were cheering. Blade guessed it was because they didn't want anyone to find out about their feelings. But why not? Blade was at a loss on the most important point.

"Oh, so no one's cheering for me?" Kassim shouted at the crowd.

The others laughed. A few of the girls drummed up the courage to shout "Kassim!" He flashed them a carefree smile in return.

"All right. Are you ready?" Blade stood between the two teams, one arm raised. "No matter who wins, no hard feelings, okay?"

Clay and Kassim had trained hard, but Blade knew there was only so much they could accomplish in a few days. For that reason, he'd focused on their consciousness and the way they sensed their power—the kinds of things you could really change a lot in a short time.

Clay had always been capable of controlling his fighting force, but he wasn't fully cognizant of it. Blade spelled out for him what fighting force was, and now he could consciously use it.

As an assassin, Kassim was more gifted in the realm of magic than in spirit, so Blade taught him how to knead his elemental power. Now he could infuse his knives with wind magic, allowing them to release blade-like gusts.

"Okay, here we go. Is everyone okay to start?"

This match would continue until one side was dead, so there was no need for a referee. But someone had to give the signal at the start and end of the fight, and that role naturally fell to Blade.

"Now... Begin!"

Blade swung his arm downward, and the battle got underway.

The first to make a move was Yessica. Spreading open her fan, she lunged recklessly forward, leaping at the two men. She trusted her partner to restore whatever slight damage she received.

It looked like today would be a two-on-two match. That was the case last time, too, but in fact it had been more like a pair of one-on-one duels—Claire versus Clay, and Yessica versus Kassim.

Yessica had recently traded in her old fan for one made of magic metal, which could conduct spirit and magic at an unusually high level. It was the latest creation from Eliza Maxwell of the academy's Research Club.

The fan suddenly emitted a warm red glow, and Clay cried out as he dodged it. Sparks of fire burst from the weapon, blinding him.

Yessica's fan was currently infused with elemental power—specifically of the fire element. Kassim braced himself, a knife in each hand as he faced off against her. That was a mistake. He was so concerned with Yessica that he'd completely forgotten about Claire.

"Yaaah!"

"*Geeeh!*"

Claire came in from the side with her morning star—a bone-crushing blow, if it struck home. Kassim just barely caught it with his weapon.

Fighting force clashed with fighting force, twisting and warping the air around them. A metallic screech could be heard even though their weapons weren't directly touching each other.

Oh? Blade noticed something.

Claire seemed to have mastered fighting force. And didn't Yessica just use elemental power? Flame, judging by the color.

"What do you think?" asked Earnest, standing next to him. "They've gotten even stronger, haven't they?"

Blade cast a sidelong glance at her. She wore a smug smile. But why?

The girls rapidly took turns, alternating between their two opponents every few seconds. Now Claire was taking on Clay.

"Yah! Yah! Yah!"

She swung her morning star, twirling the weapon and its spiky iron ball as easily as if it were a walking stick. She used it to strike at three points—the wrists, the elbows, and the shoulders.

"Argh!"

The weapon crushed one of Clay's arms, bending it in three places so it looked like it was made of rubber. Nevertheless, he fought back, swinging his sword with his other arm.

Soon, however, his sword was caught by Yessica's metal fan. She had already stepped in to oppose him.

Too bad he couldn't use fighting force to defend himself. If he could, no spiky metal ball would be able to destroy his arm like that. Sadly, they hadn't had enough training time to develop such skills. It was relatively easy to channel fighting force into a weapon, but using it to strengthen one's own body was much more difficult. Yessica was managing to use her fighting force for both offense and defense, but that was only thanks to the unique properties of her fan weapon.

"*Urgh!*"

Kassim groaned as he took a clean hit to the stomach. He fell forward with a guttural grunt as Claire came in and struck him with all her might.

"Hyah!"

"Ungh!"

Kassim fell to the ground with a pathetic whimper, the remains of his head now censored for everyone except Blade. To one side, his now head-less body twitched erratically.

That was all it took to end things when fighting a human opponent. By this point, they could no longer get back up and continue the fight. Some nonhuman foes could keep going even without a head, though, so you had to be careful. Kassim, it seemed, was human, so that was the end for him.

Clay was still going, but he only had one good arm, and he was now outnumbered.

"Claire! Leave this to me!" shouted Yessica. She was sending Claire out of the fight and making this a one-on-one battle. Incidentally, Blade felt pretty sure that by "this," she meant the kill.

"Haaah!"

Yessica went on the offensive, channeling elemental power into her fan as she attacked in a circular motion. A radiant blue light arced around her as she performed a charming, dance-like movement. Then the elemental power changed color from blue to green—from ice to wind. Then it turned red for flame, yellow for lightning, and tan for earth. The cycle continued unabated, a spectrum of energy that dazzled the audience.

First, she froze Clay's broken arm; then a barrage of wind blades tore up his body; the flames burned him up; the lightning jolted through him… And still he refused to give up. This was a far cry from Kassim, who had thrown in the towel and started twitching after losing only his head.

Yeah… Next time he got the chance, Blade would have to teach these two how to defend themselves.

Clay's good looks had been completely ruined, yet he bravely stepped forward. One of his eyeballs had been boiled in the socket and popped out, and the other was frozen solid, but the latter was still fixed firmly on Yessica.

"I'm sorry," she said coldly.

Then, with a flash of her fan—infused with steely fighting force—she exhibited a newfound expertise in the art of amputation. Clay's head rocketed into the air. By the time it hit the ground, Yessica had already turned away and folded up her fan.

Blade was probably the only one to notice the satisfied smile on Clay's face as his head soared through the sky.

Oh, right, Clay was in love with Yessica, wasn't he?

Blade was increasingly perplexed by this other kind of love...

○ Scene VII: The Postmortem

Eventually, everyone left the virtual world and returned to reality.

Clay and Kassim, who had returned a little earlier, looked both troubled and embarrassed. They each held out their hands as Yessica and Claire approached.

"We're utterly defeated," they said.

It was clear from their refreshed smiles that they had both given their all.

Yessica shook Kassim's hand, while Claire clasped Clay's with both of hers.

Wait. Hang on, that's not the right combo. Kassim liked Claire, and Clay liked Yessica, but the girls didn't seem to have picked that up.

"We'll keep getting stronger," the boys said, both grinning sheepishly.

"Please do," said the girls. "I mean, neither of us are dedicated fighters. Let's make this the last time, okay?"

The junior and senior classes both watched as the four of them shook hands.

What Blade had already noticed was now clear to everyone—the girls had undergone special training, too. Everyone could see they'd worked hard so they could beat the boys into a pulp one last time and fully destroy their pride.

Being so completely defeated a second time had truly humbled them. They could no longer kid themselves and try to claim that as boys, they had to be stronger than the girls. Now *they* were the ones trying desperately to catch up.

Blade had known it was possible that having their pride crushed might ruin the two of them for good. But that was a matter of faith. Yessica and Claire had believed in Kassim and Clay—that they would rally and recover.

"Hey." Blade nudged Sophie, who was standing beside him.

"Yes?"

"Did you teach her how to use ice elemental power?"

"I did. The other girls helped, too."

Blade followed Sophie's gaze and saw the senior-class girls standing side by side. *Ah, yes,* he thought. *That's all seven colors.*

"Is that really fair?" Clay whined. "It feels like everyone ganged up on us."

Earnest shouted, "What do you mean?!" and pointed a finger at him, wiping the wry smile right off Clay's face. "*You* had a super-being tutoring you! Don't talk to me about fairness! And besides," she continued, now in a full rage, "I've got something to say to you two!"

Clay and Kassim knelt before her.

"I don't want to hear any whining about how you have to be stronger than the girls to confess to them," Earnest said. "That's crap! If that were true, I'd never be able to fall in love!"

Blade looked on, his face blank.

Episode 3: Dueling the King

○ Scene I: The Headmaster's Office in the Morning

Knock, knock.

Flicking her wrist, Earnest knocked on the door to the headmaster's office.

Knock, knock.

"Your Majesty? Sire? Are you in there? It's Earnest Flaming."

She tried raising her voice a little, but there was still no answer. Then, just as she was about to try the doorknob—

"Gil is still resting."

"Oh! Prime Minister…"

—a woman appeared from behind the door, and Earnest straightened up to address her. This woman, in her in holy vestments, was the kingdom's prime minister. When the king was out goofing around—or rather, attending to matters of pressing concern—she was left in charge of the country. If Earnest took a high-ranking government position in the future, as she planned, the prime minister would be her boss.

"Oh no," she said, after giving Earnest a once-over.

"Did I…do something wrong?" Earnest replied, growing even more humble and polite.

Earnest found people like Sirene, women twice her age, to be the most difficult to interact with.

"It's all right to be more casual, you know. Haven't you been losing some of your stiffness around the king recently? I thought you were making progress."

Her gentle hands reached out, touching Earnest's neck, shoulders, and back.

"Wow…"

Earnest felt all the tension leave her body. It loosened her up, making it impossible to remain bolt upright. Was this some kind of martial art? A secret technique, perhaps? Whatever it was, it forcibly relaxed her in an instant. Earnest had never experienced anything like it.

"Gil is still in his bedroom. Would you mind waking him up for me?"

"Oh… Certainly."

Only now did she notice that Prime Minister Sirene had nicknamed His Majesty "Gil." *Wow,* she thought. *That's so grown-up…!*

○ Scene II: The King's Bedchamber

The king's bedroom was on the academy grounds, in a different building. Earnest approached and knocked on the door.

"Sire? It's Earnest Flaming, Your Majesty. It's morning. Are you up yet?"

She waited and waited, but no answer came. Then again, if he was answering the door, Prime Minister Sirene probably wouldn't have asked her to wake him up.

"I'm…coming in…"

The door was unlocked, so Earnest cracked it open and stealthily poked her head in. She wasn't wholly sure she was allowed to enter the king's bedroom…but if she didn't, she'd never complete the "mission" the prime minister had given her. So in she went.

The first thing that struck her was the aroma. At first, she thought it was coming from a wild animal, but she soon realized it was simply the smell of a man's body, filling the room. Ein and Zwei smelled like that, and so did horses, for that matter. It didn't strike her as particularly unpleasant.

His Majesty's bedroom was plain and unadorned. The large bed stood out, but otherwise, there was nothing but a shower room and a miniature bar for preparing drinks. The neat rows of liquor bottles provided another masculine touch. Earnest almost laughed at the idea of His Majesty mixing drinks before realizing it was probably Sirene who took care of such things. This made her blush hard.

The king was sprawled out on the large bed, snoring heavily.

"Your Majesty. Come on, Your Majesty, please wake up."

"Mmmm... Five more minutes...," he mumbled.

She was getting nowhere. This wasn't going to work.

"Your Majesty, please get up. I'll be in trouble if you don't."

But no matter what she said, the king wouldn't budge. He was still squirming around in bed.

"Your Majesty? Come on, Your Majesty. You're hopeless, aren't you?"

Starting to find humor in the situation, Earnest climbed onto the bed and started shaking him.

"Hee-hee-hee! You little scamp...," the king muttered. Then he gave her a big bear hug.

"Eek! Y-Your Majesty!"

Earnest panicked. She struggled, but the king was a former champion, and a grown man to boot. Once caught in his arms, she had no hope of escape. And now he was squeezing her.

"Your Majesty! Hey! Your Majesty! Y-you're making a mistake! It's me! Earnest Flaming!"

"Huh?" The king's eyes finally opened. "Oh, it's you, Earnest."

"I-if you recognize me, then please let go!"

He was still squeezing her, his enormous face right next to hers, as she made her flustered request.

"Oh! Sorry, sorry."

Earnest scurried away the moment she was freed from his strong arms. She took refuge in a corner of the room, her heart still pounding.

"Sorry, sorry. Guess I had the wrong idea."

"Y-yes, you did... That was quite startling," Earnest said as she fixed her hair.

It had come as a surprise, but she wasn't too upset. It had reminded her of the powerful hugs her father used to give her. He hadn't hugged her like that since she became Asmodeus's owner at age six, so the memory must have been from even further back.

Earnest glanced at the king. She could see his muscular chest, thick with hair. Apparently, he slept in the nude.

"I must say, it's quite nice to have a young girl like you wake me up."

"Wh-what's *that* supposed to mean?"

"Would you like to become one of my consorts, maybe?"

"Wh-what the heck are you *saying*?!"

Earnest almost reached for her sword before stopping herself. A move like that could be seen as treason.

"Ah-ha-ha! You're too young by five years anyway."

The king guffawed, but Earnest suspected that in five years, he might really invite her. She was growing increasingly concerned.

"I would like to serve you with my *fighting* expertise, Your Majesty!"

"Right. I expect great things from you... You may go."

"Yes, my lord."

"Or did you want to watch me get dressed?"

"I'm leaving, my lord!"

Indignant, Earnest exited the king's bedchamber.

○ Scene III: The Usual Lunch

Earnest's gang was eating lunch as normal, at their usual table in the dining hall. Everyone was enjoying the buffet, tucking into their personal favorites and eating their fill.

"Hey, listen! Hey! Hey!"

Earnest was stuffing food into her mouth as she tried to get Yessica to pay attention to what she was saying. Yessica, meanwhile, was doing an impressive job keeping up a conversation with Claire at the same time.

Blade was having his usual katsu curry. He sat with Cú on his lap, enjoying a peaceful lunchtime. Occasionally his daughter would open her mouth and say, "Ahhh," and he'd toss a piece of pork cutlet inside. If any curry was stuck to it, he'd have to lick it off first, because spicy food made Cú breathe fire, incinerating anything in front of her.

"This morning, I was squeezed by His Majesty," said Earnest.

"Wow, really?" Yessica replied casually. Three seconds later, however, she whipped back around to face Earnest, aghast. *"What?"*

"This morning, Sirene sent me to rouse him, so I went into his room, and before he fully woke up, he gave me a big bear hug."

"W-wow…" Yessica nodded a good five times at this.

For some reason, she turned to look at Blade, who was busy feeding Cú. The king was the last thing on his mind. She sighed. "…How was it?"

"Huh? It wasn't anything. He smelled like some kind of beast."

"Ewww."

"Huh?" Claire said, joining in. "What's up? Are we talking about animals? Anything furry or fuzzy?" It seemed she had no idea what they were discussing.

"Say," said Earnest, "if we're comparing that guy to an animal, what do you think he'd be?" Lately, she'd started referring to the king as "that guy," which was extremely disrespectful.

Yessica thought for a moment. "People call him the Lion Monarch, but…"

"A sleeping lion, maybe," said Earnest. "He *never* wakes up."

"Is that like a big stuffed animal?" asked Claire.

Earnest was talking about a man who smelled like a wild beast, while Claire was going on about plushies. They seemed to be on completely different pages, but in Blade's experience, girls' conversations were often like that.

"So, Anna, he hugged you while he was half-asleep, huh? How was it?" Yessica asked again.

"Like I told you, it wasn't anything. Although…maybe it was kind of nice?"

"Oh? Nice, you say?"

"It reminded me of how my father used to hug me."

"Oh, okay. Sounds like a typical reaction. You're both the right ages, too. Of course. Yeah. So *that's* what you meant. Makes sense." Yessica glanced at Blade again.

"I love stuffed animals," said Claire. "I had some pretty big ones back home, but the academy is really strict about what you can bring, so I had to leave them behind."

She was still going. She probably hadn't even noticed she was on a different page from everyone else.

"Stuffed animals? You mean the kind you hug and stuff?"

Now Earnest was showing an interest in Claire's topic. The whole conversation was beginning to fall apart.

"You can do more than just hug them. You can curl up in their arms, too. I have some so big you can sit against them, and their arms come to right about here…"

"Wow, that sounds amazing. Bring one back next time."

"I said I can't."

"Then have the king amend the constitution for you. Something like 'girls are allowed to include stuffed animals in their personal possessions.'"

"I feel like a change in the dorm rules would cover it… No need to involve the constitution."

Now plushies had become the main topic of conversation. Claire had completely taken over. In this light, you might say she was the most powerful one in the group.

Blade stood up from his seat, his plate of curry in hand. This topic was of no interest to him.

"Hey, Blade." Yessica looked at him slyly. "Are you finished already? You still have pork and curry left."

"Yeah, but I don't have much of an appetite. Here, Cú, say 'ahh.'"

"Ahhhh…"

He tossed a few slices of pork cutlet into Cú's mouth, and her cheeks ballooned out like a chipmunk's.

○ Scene IV: The Usual Training

That afternoon's class involved training in the Second Proving Ground—not virtual, but physical.

Virtual training allowed the students to crush and kill all they wanted, but it didn't build up their bodies at all. You could do thousands of push-ups in virtual reality, and you'd still be just as weak in real life.

For that reason, around half of the students' practical training was undertaken in the Second Proving Ground, where they had to actually move and work up a sweat. In the past, the girls had resented how sweaty they got during training. But ever since the thermae was built, these complaints had largely disappeared. After all, there was nothing like a good soak after training.

"Honored Father! Play with me!"

The Second Proving Ground was surrounded by a coliseum-like structure for spectators, and Cú was in her usual spot in the stands. She'd wait until the moment class was over, then fly over and tackle Blade. If he weren't an ex-Hero, the force would have killed him.

"Class is still in session," he said.

"But you're not doing anything, honored Father!"

Cú was right. Blade was leaning against the arena's fence, slacking off. He wasn't swinging his sword, and he certainly wasn't tutoring anyone. He just wasn't in the mood today, and he didn't know why. It was irritating.

He looked up at the sky and hummed in thought, trying to figure out the reason.

As he did this, Earnest approached.

"You look pretty bored, Blade. Why don't you spar with me."

"Class is still in session. The instructor's still drilling everyone."

"I know, but..." Earnest smirked just as the bell rang. "See? Class is over now!" She spun around and mustered all her dignity as the Empress to shout, "That's the end of today's classes! Dismissed!"

It was true that the school day was over. But for the Empress, ruler of the academy, there was still a lot to do. For her, regular classes were just a warm-up. Her *real* training took place afterward.

And yet today, Blade just wasn't interested.

"Sorry. It's just, I promised Cú I'd play with her, so..."

"Honored Father? You'll play with me?!" Cú sounded ecstatic.

"That's what I said, isn't it?"

"Can I bring along Ein and Zwei?"

"Sure." Blade turned back to Earnest. "So, yeah. I can't today."

"Ugh..." Earnest put a hand on her curvy hip and sighed. "All right. Then, Leonard, you spar with me."

"Yes, milady. I'd be honored."

Leonard was clearly Earnest's Plan B, but that didn't seem to bother him at all. *What a guy,* thought Blade as he waved at them and left. Cú was already dancing excitedly around him.

o **Scene V: Earnest's Invitation**

Blade and Cú touched down in the courtyard, fresh from their aerial walk. They stroked the necks of Ein and Zwei, the two spirit bird chicks, then returned them to the sky.

"See you later!"

Cú waved vigorously, swishing her tail from side to side. She was still in half-dragon mode, so the wings on her back flapped as well. The two birds circled in the air above a few times while making cute peeping noises, then flew off toward their nest atop the great spire of the royal palace.

"Oh, there you are, Blade..."

It seemed Earnest had found him again. Blade turned around, obviously uncomfortable. "H-hey."

"How are Ein and Zwei?"

"Fine. Extremely fine."

"The rest of us are gonna go to the thermae now... Why don't you come along?"

"W-well..." Blade backed away, moving behind Cú and rubbing her large wings.

"Ha-ha-ha-ha-ha! Stop tickling me, honored Father!" she exclaimed.

"You're not going?" asked Earnest. "Why not?"

"Oh... I dunno."

"But you're filthy."

Earnest had held out for a long time, reluctant to enter the mixed-gender bath. But lately, she was even inviting other people to join her.

"It's all right. I can just use the bath in my dorm room."

"Ugh..." Earnest put a hand on her hip and sighed. She got the feeling something like this had happened rather recently. "All right, I'll make do with Leonard, then. Come on, Leonard."

"Yes, milady. It's an honor to join you."

Despite obviously serving as a backup option once again, Leonard gleefully followed Earnest away. The exact same thing had happened earlier.

Blade didn't mind Leonard at all... So why did the same thing bother him so much when it was *that guy*?

Blade pondered this question as he headed back to his dorm, pulling Cú along by the hand.

○ Scene VI: The King and His Mistress

"How are they?"

At my lord's quiet question, I opened the curtains an inch or two and looked down into the courtyard.

"Young and innocent," I replied, saying exactly what I thought.

"Are you jealous?"

"No. After all, I was like that, too, once."

My lord and I had been together for many years, but even now, there were many things I didn't understand about how his mind worked.

"You always put him through so much trouble," I ventured. "Don't you think he'll tire of you sooner or later?"

I knew well, though, that if such words had the power to sway him, he would have changed long, long ago.

"He needs to enjoy his youth."

That was certainly true. Seventeen years as a Hero had stolen far too many things from that boy. Now he was finally taking them back, one at a time.

"Everything is improved by a little spice, you know?" he continued. "The same is true of love. I'm just giving him a push in the right direction."

"You make it sound like you overslept this morning on purpose."

"If that's what it looked like to you," my lord replied, "perhaps you're onto something."

Even for those of us who worked alongside him, it was sometimes hard to determine how much of what happened around him was coincidence and how much was on purpose. My lord just happened to sleep in this morning; he told me to have Earnest wake him up later, so I did. And now this had happened.

If you didn't know my lord very well, you might think all his moves were meticulously calculated. Most people in the kingdom's affiliated nations believed the Sleeping Lion Monarch was even capable of working magic. But those close to him knew the truth. His actions were, to a great extent, based on whims, moods, or passing thoughts.

He might place his faith in that boy—the Hero—and regard him as a legend, but to us, it was *my lord* who was the real legend.

It takes a great man to walk the path of conquest. Such things are not paved in advance. When a truly great individual accomplishes a truly extraordinary deed, the commonfolk see a conqueror. That is the only way such a path can be forged.

"You should go to the thermae later," my lord said as he worked through a stack of papers, signing each one. We had already reviewed and approved them, and all they needed was his signature.

"How much later would you prefer?"

"The small hours of the night, of course... Oh, and I'd like you to go alone, naturally."

An ordinary woman like me couldn't fathom what he meant by "of course" and "naturally." And so I simply nodded and said I would be there.

○ Scene VII: Passing Ships

It was dinnertime, and the students were gathered in the dining hall.

"Oh, Blade! Over here, over here!"

Earnest was waving from their usual table. But Blade ignored her and kept walking.

"I've got homework tonight," he said. "I'll eat in my dorm room."

"Huh? Homework? But you've always ignored that stuff... Whoa! Blade! Wait a minute!"

Earnest's voice grew more and more distant as Blade left her behind.

Sometime after that, the two of them bumped into each other in the hallway.

"Oh, hey, Blade," said Earnest. "I'm hosting a girls' night... You wanna join us?"

"Nah. Isn't that kind of thing just for girls?"

"What? But that never stopped you before... Hey! Where are you going?"

"Number two."

"Ugh... Just go, you idiot!"

Late that night, someone came to Blade's door.

"Hey... Are you in there, Blade?"

By the time Earnest knocked, Blade was already out of bed. He quickly opened his window and threw himself outside.

"What is your prob— *Arghhh!*"

Earnest stormed into Blade's dorm room, but the boy himself was nowhere to be found. This was the last straw.

Cú alone was in the bed, sleeping soundly. Meanwhile, the window was wide open, its curtains fluttering in the breeze.

"No! No, all right? It's not *like* that! ...You want me to snap you in half?!"

The sword hanging from her hip was saying something rude again, no doubt. Earnest proceeded to take all her inscrutable anger out on the weapon.

○ Scene VIII: The Thermae

Blade had managed to escape out the window, but he didn't have anywhere to go, so he decided to flee into the thermae. Even alone, once he got his clothes off, he could relax and enjoy the hot water.

"Ha-ha! There's four of them."

The large and small moon were reflected on the water's surface, making it look like there were four out—two above, and two below. Something about that struck Blade as funny. He splashed a bit, lowering the count back to two, but before long, there were four again. After repeating this a few times, he sensed someone approaching from behind.

"Sophie?" he said, turning around to find a bored-looking blue-haired girl. Her silhouette was slender with few curves, and her wet hair lay flat against her head, changing the shape of her face slightly.

Sophie, standing there in her birthday suit, raised an eyebrow. "...How did you know it was me?"

"Oh, just a hunch." He figured it had to be Sophie, since she seemed to always be there for him when he was in trouble. "But how did you know *I'd* be here?"

"Because you're always in the thermae at this time of night."

Blade chuckled. It seemed he'd been overly self-conscious. For a moment, he'd thought Sophie was going out of her way to pamper him.

"I… I guess I'm feeling a little irritated right now," Blade admitted. "…Though I'm not sure why."

He could always be honest with Sophie. He never felt the need to hide anything from her.

"I've noticed you avoiding Earnest lately," she said.

"Huh? Avoiding her? …Really?"

"Yes, really."

If Sophie said so, it had to be true. And now that he thought about it, it made sense. Recently, he'd had a hard time looking Earnest in the face. So…maybe he *had* been running away.

"Yeah… Maybe you're right." Blade nodded. He was sure of it now. "But why am I avoiding her?"

"Well, why are you feeling irritated?"

"I don't know," Blade said. If he knew, he wouldn't be having this problem.

"For that matter, when you say you're irritated, what does that mean, exactly?"

"We have to start from there?" Blade groaned.

Come to think of it, Sophie had never been great with understanding emotions. Blade knew he had trouble comprehending regular people's feelings, but Sophie was even worse at it than he was. No matter how much common sense he lacked as an ex-Hero, he still knew what being "irritated" meant.

How should I explain it…? Blade thought for a moment—or rather, he tried to. But soon, a voice interrupted him.

"Are you familiar with the word…'jealousy'?"

"Huh?"

"…?!"

Blade and Sophie turned their heads at the same time. The voice had come from only a few yards away. Blade gasped, while Sophie leaped a foot or so back and assumed a battle stance. Both of them—an ex-Hero and an artificial Hero—had been taken completely by surprise.

The speaker—a grown woman—was pouring water over her shoulders. Her hair was put up, giving her head quite a lot of volume. It was Sirene, the kingdom's prime minister. When did she show up? How long had she been there?

Sophie's hair bristled, while Blade's heart raced. Neither of them had sensed the prime minister at all. If she had been there from the beginning, she hadn't just eluded them—she'd deceived their very senses!

Her breasts sure were large, though… Blade had never taken any special interest in the opposite sex before. But recently, following his sudden discovery of lips, he had come to understand a little more about breasts as well. In the past, these rounded objects had never really concerned him even when they came into view. Recently, though, he had noticed his gaze gravitating toward them.

While the others were teaching him how to swim, Sophie had given him a hefty dose of her breasts, and he'd buried his face in Claire's as well. He got the feeling that experience had put him on the cusp of understanding something. In fact, maybe he already qualified as a "boobmeister."

Blade looked at Sirene's breasts, then Sophie's, comparing them. The prime minister's were at least three times bigger—maybe five. He thought Sirene's could definitely fit at least five of Sophie's inside.

"I think," Sophie said as Blade's head bobbed back and forth between them, "I am starting to understand what 'irritation' is."

"Huh? What? Why?" Blade asked.

Sirene snickered, a graceful hand covering her mouth. Unlike Blade's female classmates, a grown woman like her didn't giggle loudly or cackle like a hyena.

"It seems it's still too early for 'jealousy,'" Sirene said, smiling.

Then she stood up from the water. The rest of her body was graceful and mature—especially that dark-colored patch. Her legs moved back and forth as she walked away. Blade watched her toned rear end as it disappeared into the steam.

"Jealousy… So what is it, huh? What's it like?" Blade was still poring over the words she'd left behind. "Do you know, Sophie?"

The two of them—both beginners at emotions—looked at each other and shook their heads. The gentle smile faded from Sophie's face, and she fell silent for a moment. Then, as she stared at the surface of the water, a few words escaped her mouth.

"Blade... Can I ask you a question?"

"Mmm? What's up?"

"If I was the one who got bear-hugged by the king, what would you have thought about that?"

"Huh?"

"If was me, not Earnest, being squeezed, what would you do?"

"What would I do? Um..."

"Would you still be jealous?"

"What?"

"I'm sorry. Forget about it."

"Huh? Huuuh? Huuuuuh?" Blade blinked helplessly. Was "jealousy" the cause of his recent irritability...? "No way."

Come on. That's crazy.

He'd finally remembered. He once read in the dictionary that *jealousy* was the feeling of wanting to completely monopolize someone. As Earnest's friend, Blade wanted her to be happy, but he'd never wanted to occupy all her time...

Besides, none of this made any sense. He didn't even understand this special sort of "love" other people supposedly felt... At least not that he was aware of.

"Blade," said Sophie "...I don't care if what you're feeling is jealousy or not."

"......"

Blade clammed up and stared at the water.

"But Blade... What do you want to do?"

At that, he raised his head. "I..."

○ Scene IX: Waiting

Wind blew across the riverbank, dyed red in the evening sun.

Blade was waiting, his arms folded and a frown on his face. He had been standing there, amid the swaying grass, waiting for a certain man to appear.

They had agreed to meet at sunset by the river. Things like this had always taken place at such times and locations, even in the distant past. Knowing this, Blade had made sure to follow the proper etiquette.

The grass began swaying in a different direction. The other person had finally arrived, so Blade turned around.

"Hey," said the newcomer. "Sorry I'm late."

"Yeah, you sure are," Blade grumbled.

"I never thought you'd confess to me like this."

"Huh? Who the heck is confessing? What are you, stupid?" That wasn't why Blade had called this meeting. And what was he supposed to "confess"? He hadn't done anything.

He fixed his opponent—the king—with a threatening glare full of murderous intent.

"Dione, you're willing to serve as witness?" asked the king.

"Yes, my lord! Witnessing this duel between the He—er, Blade—and Your Majesty is a great honor! I, Dione of the Magic Spear, shall have yet another heart-pounding story to take with me to Valhalla!"

"Why's she so excited?" asked Blade.

"I told her we were going to have a duel, and she said she'd slit her own throat unless she was allowed to observe."

"You should have let her do it."

Blade was at a loss. What were all these people doing here? He looked around at the hundreds of audience members gathered to watch. There were students from the academy, as well as townspeople, standing around on the embankment. Women were pointing at him and telling their children "See? That's the man who rebuilt our house!" They were wrong, of course. It was the spirit bird, the simurgh, who destroyed those houses, and the king who rebuilt them.

"The bigger the audience, the better, I say," said the king. "I went ahead and sent out an official notice with the time and place."

"Hah! You want this many people to see you lose?" Blade spat.

Spewing lines like that was making Blade start to feel like a third-rate villain… That was exactly what such a character would say, and now *he'd* said it.

When Sophie asked him what he wanted to do, his first impulse was to punch this guy good and hard.

Why? What for?

Because he'd given Earnest a bear hug. That was enough—a crime deserving of a thousand deaths. It wasn't a matter of "jealousy"—he was just pissed off.

Right. Yeah. Pissed off. That's all. That was more than enough reason to throw hands.

"Blade!"

A red figure jumped out from the crowd of onlookers. Earnest ran down the bank with Leonard in tow. They were headed straight for Blade.

"Stay back!" Blade shouted.

It was true that this had all started because of Earnest, but it no longer involved her. At this point, it was simply a clash of wills between two men.

"Why are you picking a fight with His Majesty? I don't get it, but…are you stupid or something?"

"Milady…"

Leonard's eyes were filled with pity, and they were pointed straight at Blade. The ex-Hero felt all the blood vessels in his brain tensing.

Man, I can't let this go on. If I don't punch that guy good and hard, this feeling will never stop.

"Wait, Blade—!"

"Milady…" Leonard pulled Earnest away.

"Surely this can't be the case," said the king, "but I'll ask anyway. Do you truly intend to beat me? You're at under fifteen percent of your prime, and you think you can win?"

"Hah! I can take on one or two decrepit old champions without even breaking a sweat."

He was an ex-Hero, and he wasn't going to be underestimated. In fact, it seemed presumptuous to suggest he wouldn't win, even at 15 percent.

"Then allow me to show you why I am called the Lion Monarch."

It was true that the king was known by that name, and the reason... Well, Blade had never actually heard why.

"Among lions, males do none of the work," he continued. "The females do all the hunting."

"What?"

A group of women came out from behind the king. They weren't in their usual clothes, either. They were fully decked out in battle gear.

They were equipped with the weapons and armor they'd used during the great war, when they'd served as the king's guard and made up the kingdom's most elite force. Nearly all of their equipment was legendary-class— banned during peacetime by the Six-Nation Treaty.

"Huh? What?! Whoa...!"

Blade panicked.

Meanwhile, the group of twelve semi-champions quickly surrounded him. Blade had no intention of losing to a decrepit old champion, but as for these twelve women... If he could break out 50 percent, it'd be a different story. But with only 15 percent? He wasn't so sure.

Sirene was smiling at him, a thorn whip in her hands. *Didn't I specify that I wanted a one-on-one duel?! I know I did!*

"All you said was 'I'll be waiting for you by the river,'" said the king. "You said nothing about coming alone, and even if you had, these women are aligned with me in body and soul. In other words, all of us function as one."

The king raised one arm, then lowered it.

"Oh, come *onnnn!*" Blade shouted.

○ Scene X: After the Duel

"You idiot!"

Earnest yelled at Blade as he lay on the grass by the river, too exhausted to reply. If his concentration wavered for even a moment, he would probably lose consciousness.

He thought he'd put up a good fight, at least. A semi-champion was generally seen as around a third as powerful as a regular champion, and it was assumed that three semi-champions together could defeat a single champion. Even if the king's women hadn't been terribly serious about the duel with Blade, there were twelve of them attacking him all at once. Blade thought he deserved some praise just for not being insta-killed.

In fact, he'd managed to draw out the fight for an hour before he fell. Still, all twelve of them had ganged up and beat the crap out of him in the end. The ladies were quite cruel to him. They'd all smiled the whole time they were whaling on him. And once they were done, they'd trotted off in high spirits. True to his word, the king hadn't even lifted a finger.

"You are *such* an idiot," Earnest repeated.

"I know. Owww…"

Blade tried to sit up, but Earnest caught his head between her hands and lowered it back down into her lap.

"Let's go to the thermae later. The water's supposed to be good for healing wounds."

"I can't get up until you let go of me," Blade said.

"Okay. But I want to stay like this a while longer… That's all right, isn't it?"

"Well, fine, but…"

Earnest was smiling contentedly.

Why is she *so happy?* Leonard was watching them from afar. *Did he say something unnecessary to her?*

But as Earnest looked down at him with a big smile on her face, Blade found that all the irritation and gloom that had been plaguing him had completely disappeared.

How weird. And I didn't even manage to punch the king.

Chapter 2:
Not Quite Human

○ Scene I: In the Morning

Ka-chunk, ka-chunk.

There it was, walking along the road as dawn began to break, crushing leaves beneath its feet. It turned its single green eye to the right, then swung it to the left. No target in sight.

Currently, it was unsure what to do. It was originally designed for base security, and its mission was to unconditionally attack anyone who approached. It wasn't designed to search people out. In fact, it wasn't designed to move around that much, either.

In the end, it decided to wait. It knew from the GPS coordinates that it had reached the target's area of operation. If it stopped and waited, there was a near 100 percent probability that the target would eventually appear.

It used its two legs and two feelers to fix itself into position. Its metallic body couldn't feel fatigue. It could wait for hundreds of years without changing its posture—and now it was in standby mode.

✳

"Heff, heff, heff, heff, heff, heff..."

A few dedicated joggers passed by in the morning. They noticed the new object on the side of the road, but since they were busy training, they ignored it and moved on.

*

By the time the lunch hour rolled around, the scene was very different. A crowd of people had gathered around the object. Someone had spotted it and spread the word, and now the whole area was lined with onlookers.

Automatons, in and of themselves, were not that unusual. They saw frequent use in practical combat training, for one. But this one's design—the teardrop-shaped body, the single green eye—was pretty uncommon.

"Isn't the little robot cute? I wonder where it's from. It's just so adorable! Do you think it's waiting for somebody? It's sooo cute!"

Yessica sighed as her friend Claire made a fuss over the robot.

"It's so *smooth*!" she squealed, stroking the top of its round head.

Yessica was drawn in and put her own hand on its head. The white material felt strange to the touch—not metal, but not stone or anything else, either.

Its single large, green eye lent it a sort of charm. "Cute" might be overstating it, but it did have a kind of adorably ugly aesthetic.

"What're you people doing?" said Earnest, when she arrived on the scene.

She was a lot calmer and more casual than she'd been during her reign of terror as the Empress. As she spoke, she placed a hand on her hip—so curvaceous that even Yessica was jealous.

"Well, you see this guy?" Yessica said, patting the robot's smooth head.

"It's an automaton. So what?"

"Cute! So cuuuute!" Claire couldn't stop touching it. She was clearly out of her mind, so Yessica stepped up to explain instead.

"We were just discussing what it could be doing here."

"Come to think of it, it was here this morning, too," said Earnest.

"Wow! So it's been here awhile. I wonder who it's waiting for?" said Claire.

Yessica patted it on the head. Just then, its single eye began to glow.

"Oops... Did I turn it on?"

Light projected from the automaton's eye and formed an image in the air.

"What's that...?"

Everyone stared at the boy in the image. They all recognized him instantly.

○ Scene II: Blade

Blade was spending his lunch break in the deserted Proving Ground, meditating. It was a kind of self-training, and he'd even skipped eating his favorite katsu curry to pursue it.

Lately, he'd been experiencing a severe decline in power. In the past, he'd suffered a near-lethal wound fighting the Overlord, which had taken him several months to recover from. His doctor had subsequently informed him that he would die if he exercised even 30 percent of the power he'd had in his prime. And it turned out to be no idle threat, either. That was exactly how much he'd used in his battle against Ovie, the Overlord's daughter, and it really *had* killed him.

Since his revival, he had to stay under 15 percent—and he no longer had any doubt that he'd be done for if he pushed it. He'd be dead if he used the full 15, so the max amount of power he could tap into was 14.9 percent, which severely limited the number of skills he could use.

All of his Heroic sword skills, for example, were off the table. Out of the seven dragon-destroying techniques, Dragon Eater was the best he could manage, and that was the second weakest of the group. In his prime, he could even break out the most powerful, something it was said no one else had ever managed... But then again, if no one had ever used it, how did it get passed down through generations of Heroes? *Sounds a little fishy.*

Seeing his power dwindle didn't bother Blade at all. He was a normal person now, not a Hero, and there was no longer any need for him to win.

He didn't need to beat insurmountable foes anymore, and it wouldn't be a big deal if he easily lost to someone way more powerful than he was. He didn't need to make the impossible possible or pull off absurd moves. He'd already lost to the king's entourage not long ago.

But even if 15 percent was his currently prescribed limit, there must be an optimal way to use what power he did have. That was what Blade was searching for. For someone like him, who had always relied on his overwhelming power, this was a new discovery, a new frontier to explore. What was he capable of at 15 percent power?

"Hngh…!"

For a while now, he'd been kneading spirit and fighting force inside his body. All of a sudden, he compressed it and gathered it just below his navel. It was enough for one invocation of Dragon Eater.

He could only generate up to 15 percent of his power at any given time, but what would happen if he "charged" himself with enough energy for a single big move while not in battle?

This was, of course, the first time he'd ever tried such a thing. Gathering all the necessary energy had taken him about half an hour. But now that he had the hang of it, Blade thought he could manage it in only a few minutes.

But just as he started working on his second shot, he heard footsteps approaching.

"Is that you, Earnest?" he asked.

"What're you doing, Blade? You didn't even eat lunch."

"Well, you know…" He opened one eye. It wasn't just Earnest—all the usual girls were there, Claire and Yessica included.

"…?"

Even if they wanted to drag him back to the dining hall, they didn't need *this* many people. Was skipping his katsu curry for one day *that* big of a deal?

But it seemed Earnest was here for something else.

"Blade, I think this thing's searching for you…," she said, pushing a teardrop-shaped automaton toward him.

"…Get away," he said loudly, standing up from his full lotus position.

"Huh?"

"I said get away from that thing!"

The automaton Earnest had brought was a Guardian—a dangerous machine Blade had encountered many times in the labyrinth beneath the castle.

He readied his sword.

"Whoa! Blade…?!"

He quickly prepared the shot he had just charged—

"Instant Dragon Eater!!"

—and without any preliminary movement, Blade unleashed his technique.

"Whoa!"

The narrowly focused superhelix brushed past Earnest, Claire, Yessica, and the other girls and wrapped around the automaton's body. That kept any damage to the girls at a minimum. Yes, the helix would suck up all their clothing, but that was the worst of it.

In an instant, the Guardian was swallowed by the spiral and blown away. It spun through the air and slammed into the Proving Ground's fence, its limbs and feelers torn off by the centrifugal force.

"Whoa, Blade! What are you doing?!" Earnest's agitated voice echoed across the arena. As usual, she was the first one to mentally recover. "Why'd you attack it like that? You destroyed it!"

"Whoa! Anna! You're naked!" Yessica used her own body to cover up the now half-naked Earnest.

"Oh," Earnest said, "I didn't notice."

Recently, she'd had plenty of chances to become the Nude Avenger, and she'd been showing a lot of skin in the thermae as well, so she was growing less and less sensitive to the eyes of the opposite sex.

"This is nothing anyway," she said. "There aren't even any boys around."

I'm right here, thought Blade.

"But Blade!" Earnest shouted. "Why'd you destroy it? That poor thing! It didn't do anything, and you sent it flying!"

Earnest pointed at the Guardian, which was now throwing off sparks.

Looking at the extent of the damage, it was a total loss. Blade put his sword away, reasonably sure it wouldn't get up again, at least for a little while.

"Well, um… It's what I always do," he said.

"Huh? Are you stupid?" Earnest shot back.

"What? Always? What do you mean, 'always'?" asked Claire.

"I mean, isn't this the same one I always fight?" Blade replied, taking in Claire's blank stare. All of a sudden, something dawned on him. "Oh, right."

The Royal Forbidden Library was located in a fairly deep part of the great labyrinth beneath the palace. This Guardian was the protector of that library, and every time Blade needed to go there to look something up, he first had to get through a round of delicate negotiations—in other words, knocking this guy out of commission. That said, no one but a Hero would have much use for the Forbidden Library. Most people would never encounter this Guardian, much less have to defeat it. Of course none of Blade's classmates knew about it.

"But what's it doing way out here?" he wondered aloud.

The Guardian was supposed to keep watch over the Forbidden Library. So why was it up here on the surface?

Claire was completely flustered, her gaze moving back and forth between Blade and the Guardian, still stuck in the fence.

"Um… So you know this automaton, Blade?" she asked. "Because earlier, it showed us a picture—or maybe a photo—of you…"

"So, Blade, you really do know it?" Earnest pressed.

"Oh, great. Maybe it escalated my threat level and now it's targeting me for termination…"

"Termination? That's a little scary. What the heck did you do?"

"Well, I mean, I destroyed it a bunch of times."

"Um," said Claire, still freaking out. "Shouldn't we, you know, fix it or something? Ummm…"

"It'll fix itself if we leave it there," Blade assured her. "Ancient Guardians have an auto-repair function."

"Oh? But…ummm…"

At that point, the bell rang for afternoon classes. Blade started to walk off, and the rest of the group followed him.

Meanwhile, the Guardian stuck in the fence stared after Blade as he left, its single eye flickering and its body still spewing sparks.

○ Scene III: Auto-Repair

The automaton lay still, stuck in the fence and buried in rubble, thinking to itself. It had put its auto-repair process on hold for the time being.

It could easily use nanomachines to restore itself to its original form. Even if someone dismantled it or burned it to ashes, it could return to normal in less than a day. If some of its original form remained, the process would only be made easier.

But simply returning to its original form would not be enough to defeat its target. That had been proved time and again. It had to eliminate it. The target had destroyed the automaton many times, preventing it from performing its mission of keeping intruders out of the core block. And accomplishing its mission was the only basis for the automaton's existence.

And so it continued to ponder. What abilities would it need to defeat its target, and what form would be best? Simple repairs were not enough. It needed to *evolve*.

As it replayed a record of the last time it was destroyed on a constant loop, it eventually came to realize something. In the previous battle, the target was paying attention to how he fought—taking great care not to harm the human girls in the surrounding area. The automaton thought about the particular form of a young human girl. It felt sure a significant hint was hidden there somewhere.

Maybe…just maybe… This was simply one possibility—a mere hypothesis, but…

…was its shape the problem? Was this form wrong, somehow? What if it adopted the form of a young girl, instead?

Maybe…just maybe…the target would go a little easier on it.

And so, following this reasoning, the automaton evolved and changed its shape.

○ Scene IV: In the Afternoon

"What *was* all that yesterday? I swear…"

"What about yesterday?"

Morning training was in progress, and as usual, Blade was making small talk with Earnest as he helped her with sword practice.

Clang, clang.

They exchanged blows, switching locations like a choreographed dance. They slashed at each other, dodged blow after blow, and chatted a bit in between.

None of their moves were rehearsed, of course. The swords were real, their blades sharpened. In fact, Earnest was using her magic sword Asmodeus as is. Each of their blows, aside from the occasional feint, would have been lethal if it wasn't fully parried or avoided.

For some reason Blade couldn't fathom, nobody wanted to spar against Earnest. And so, inevitably, Blade wound up paired with her most of the time. Basically *all* the time.

"What about yesterday?" Blade asked again.

Earnest was dishing out strike after strike so fast there wasn't even time to breathe, and Blade was fending off each one of them.

Whenever Earnest executed an extended combo attack, she always fell silent for some reason Blade didn't understand.

Sounding a little out of breath, Earnest finally said, "You know… A lot of things. First, you attacking that cute little robot."

The girls had all called the Guardian "cute," or at least "adorably ugly." Blade, on the other hand, couldn't stop himself from looking at it as an opponent and was blind to everything but its battle capabilities.

It might have looked like he defeated it with ease, but the Guardian was actually a fairly troublesome opponent. The longer the battle dragged on, in fact, the trickier it became to win.

The tubelike ends of the Guardian's arms could shoot out beams of light

strong enough to blow up an entire castle. The two long feeler-like appendages snaking out from behind its back produced extremely thin wires that,
when swung forward, could cut through any material as though it were
butter. What's more, just touching the Guardian would paralyze any living creature.

Thus, the correct way to handle it was to blow it away the moment you
saw it, before it could enter battle mode.

"Also, what was that skill you used?!" said Earnest.

"What skill?" Blade asked, his sword clanging as he parried Earnest's
slashes. It seemed like she was even more murderous than usual today.

"That skill, the one that was like Dragon Eater!"

"It wasn't 'like' anything. That *was* Dragon Eater."

"How did you shoot it without any windup?! That thing usually takes
a while to charge, doesn't it?!"

"Oh, right. About that…" Instead of catching Earnest's sword, Blade
leaped away, then swung in a wide arc and on a whim shouted, "Instant
Dragon Eater!"

He fired his skill straight up, and a superhelix of spirit and fighting force
spiraled toward the ceiling of the Second Proving Ground.

The attack bounced off the magic barrier, was deflected and changed
course a few more times, then finally dissipated. All it did was stir the air
around them a little and raise the temperature in the Proving Ground by
a few degrees.

"What're you doing?! Ugh! You're so stupid! You scared me!"

Earnest was raging at him again—and come to think of it, Dragon
Eater *did* catch her a little the day before. *But that's exactly why I was careful! I made sure it only affected her clothes, and it worked. I thought I did
pretty well, actually.*

"Yesterday, I figured it out—a way to do it without charging. I just have
to prepare the energy beforehand and keep it handy, and then I can use it
right away, just like any old normal technique."

"'Normal'…? What's normal about that? It's so powerful!"

"But it *is* normal. The barrier even repelled it and everything."

Blade pointed a finger upward. The normal strength of the magic barrier constantly surrounding the Second Proving Ground was good enough to block Dragon Eater. It hadn't ripped a hole in the ceiling or anything.

When he'd first arrived at the academy, his Dragon Eater had taken out not only the wall but the adjacent school building, too. Thanks to that, the barrier's "normal strength" was now quite high.

"This new strategy is pretty handy. I wish I'd figured it out a long time ago. I can even do rapid fire."

"Rapid fire…? Um…how many…shots can you manage?"

"I think I can store up to six uses at a time," Blade answered.

After the incident with the automaton the day before, he had continued meditating until he charged up enough energy for six shots. He had used one of them just now, but the other five were still in the chamber, so to speak. Dividing one hundred by fifteen came to a little over six—apparently that was how the math worked.

"Six…"

Earnest was stunned into silence, though Blade wasn't sure why.

Back in his Hero days, Dragon Eater was basically useless against most of the enemies he encountered… But now that he was a normal student, it was about the best he could do. Still, it wasn't anything special. If he worked it right, it was clearly possible to fire it six times without even charging. He'd simply never thought about it before.

Back in the day, he'd always had to conserve his mental and physical energy, just in case he had to fire off something big in a pinch. Charging up smaller moves in advance would leave no room for bigger finishers later. But thanks to his new 15 percent limit, Dragon Eater was the best he could do; nothing more powerful was available. If he tried busting out the *real* big guns, he'd be dead. So Blade decided to keep six shots of Dragon Eater ready to go at all times whenever possible.

"Mm? What's the matter, Earnest?"

"I'm just stunned."

"Why?"

"Well… I guess there's no point, is there? If I keep letting you shock and stun me with everything you do, I'll lose my mind. You *are* a super-being, after all."

"I told you to knock that off."

That kind of treatment was starting to feel like discrimination. She'd cornered this poor, wimpy ex-Hero who could barely use 15 percent of his power, and now she was calling him a "super-being"? There ought to be a law against treating people like this.

"Why don't *you* knock it off?" she asked. "All your crazy nonsense, that is..."

"Look, I'll teach you, okay? I'll teach all of you. Everybody here can pull this off, trust me. All you gotta do is knead your spirit like a ball of dough and mix in some fighting force. You compress it, and then you wring it out and compress it again... See? It's easy."

"Sure. Yeah. Easy."

It seemed Earnest had given up protesting. She lifted one arm and flicked her wrist a few times, motioning for him to go away. Blade puffed out his cheeks in indignation.

"...So, um, did you notice that?" he asked.

"I did," Earnest replied. "What do you think is going on?"

The two of them turned to the side. The fence Blade had thrown the Guardian into the day before was now a pile of rubble. The automaton's remains should have been buried among them...but instead, there was a long-haired girl sitting atop the pile. She was staring down at them from one of the larger rocks. She clearly wasn't a student—Blade and Earnest knew everyone at the academy. Up until a few weeks ago, there were a few holes in Blade's memory, but after some training courtesy of Cú, he now had every name down pat.

There definitely wasn't anyone with green hair enrolled at the academy. She wasn't wearing a uniform, either. Her body was wrapped in a suit made of some unfamiliar material. At first, Blade thought it was some sort of armor, but it showed off quite a bit of skin. Blade wasn't sure if the outfit was meant for combat or for showing off the wearer's limbs. She wore a hair accessory that looked like some kind of machine part.

"…Do you know her?" asked Earnest.

"Hmm…"

Blade *did* feel like he recognized her from somewhere, but he wasn't quite sure. A few elements looked familiar, like that big green round part on her hair accessory…

The girl locked eyes with Blade, then jumped down from her perch and approached the two of them.

Once she was close enough, she asked Blade, "How do you like this body?"

She put her weight on one leg as she showed off her slender form. She brushed back her hair with one hand and twisted her upper body slightly, as if showing it off.

Blade didn't know a lot about such things, but it seemed to him that she was particularly well proportioned.

"Hey!" said Blade, addressing the men in the area. "She's asking what you think about her body!"

His eyes were especially on Leonard and Kassim, as well as Clay, who acted serious but was pretty perverted on the inside. All of them stared at the green-haired girl's body.

"…Seems they all like what they see," said Blade.

Claire whapped Clay on the back of the head, and Yessica did the same to Kassim. Earnest went for Leonard, but she opted for a murderous thrust that would've cut him in half had he not managed to dodge.

"Yes. I am sure they do. I analyzed the male human psyche to design a look that would inspire their protective instincts. With this appearance, I have the highest probability of being chosen as the ideal breeding partner. My chest armor is 1.83 times thicker than the average for females. It must be overwhelming."

Blade had no idea what she was talking about, but he glanced at the other boys to gauge their reactions.

"…You heard her," he said. He felt certain she was fishing for compliments. Then Blade turned back to the girl, deciding it was finally time to ask the question that had been bothering him all this time. "By the way, who are you?"

The girl smiled at him. "You do not know who I am?"

"That's kinda why I'm asking…"

"I have attained new heights of self-improvement. My transformation is so great, you need not feel embarrassed for not recognizing me."

"Are you even listening?"

The girl was still smiling, but to Blade, she now looked smug.

"You seem surprised that we are able to communicate via language as well. However, with my high-spec functionality, learning spoken human languages is a breeze."

"Actually, I'm not surprised at all. I'm just asking who the heck you are."

"Hey… Um, Blade?" Claire was pulling at his sleeve.

"Yeah?"

"This person…er, this girl… Isn't she the one from before?"

"Huh? Who do you mean?" Blade looked at her, confused.

"Oh, I get it. The one from before," said Yessica.

Blade turned to look at her. "Huh? You know what Claire's talking about?"

"Oh, man, were we just…?" It seemed Leonard, Clay, and Kassim had figured it out, too. But why did they look so depressed?

"Guys, guys, tell me!" shouted Blade. "Stop picking on me like this."

"Hee-hee! Wow, Blade, you really don't know?" Earnest was enjoying every moment of this. *Why is she always so mean to me?*

But Blade knew who to ask next—someone who was always on his side.

"Hey, Sophie, do *you* know?"

Sophie looked at the new girl for a moment, then turned back to Blade. After a moment's pause, she said, "The Guardian…maybe?" Her head was tilted a good forty-five degrees as she spoke, and she didn't sound too sure of herself.

"What? Are you kidding? There's no way." Blade slapped Sophie on the back a few times. "How can the Guardian be—"

But then he took a closer look at the girl. She *did* seem familiar. Like that round green part on her hair accessory, for example.

Wait. Huh? Huuuh? Huuuuuh?!

"You! You're the Guardian!" he exclaimed.

"I see you have finally recognized me. I am not surprised it took you so long. That is how perfect my mimicry is. For example, look at the texture of my skin. It is completely identical to that of a real woman's body, down to the organic material that composes its tissue."

The girl—the Guardian—took Blade's hand and pressed it—palm and all—against her breast. He had buried his face in a pair of breasts before, but he had never touched any with his hands, so there was no way for Blade to judge how "realistic" they were. As far as he was concerned, with his wrist in the Guardian's grasp, there was only one thing for him to do.

"Dragon Eater!!"

Because he wasn't carrying a weapon, he wasn't able to focus his energy well. The attack blew the Guardian away but fizzled out before causing any real damage.

Once he'd sent her flying, he took out his sword and began to unleash even more attacks, this time at full power.

"Dragon Eater! Dragon Eater! Dragon Eater!"

He let loose three strikes in rapid succession. When used like this, Dragon Eater seemed less and less impressive.

"Whoa! Blade?!" shouted Earnest.

Debris flew through the air, earth and sand fell over them, and clouds of dust rose up from the ground. Blade peered through all this and saw that the Guardian was still partially intact, so he gave it one more shot for good measure.

"Dragon Eaterrrrr!!"

That finally did the job. The Guardian's body was completely pulverized.

"Wow… That was close." Blade relaxed and wiped the sweat from his forehead.

"Like I was saying! What are you *doing*, Blade?!" shouted Earnest as she whapped him in the back of the head with her sword's scabbard. *Why is she being so mean?*

"What am I doing? Well, I sent the thing flying."

"Yeah, we saw that! But I'm asking *why* you sent her flying!"

"That was the Guardian, wasn't it?"

"But she was a girl!"

"Yeah, but she was the Guardian, wasn't she?"

"Why did you destroy her?!"

Earnest wasn't alone. Everyone's reproachful gaze was now on Blade. *Do they not realize how menacing the Guardian is? No, I guess they don't. They never fought on the front lines like I did or plunged into the underground labyrinth.*

Fortunately, the Guardian was still fixated on eliminating Blade, but sometimes these things would lose control and revert to their true murderous nature, becoming something called a "berserker." Out in the fringes, everyone was terrified of them.

"You're so merciless, Blade!"

"Yeah! That poor girl!"

"They're right, Blade," said Kassim. "That was such a waste— Um, I mean, that was so mean of you." He'd almost let slip what all the boys were thinking.

"Didn't you all see what happened last time? It won't be gone for long."

No matter how many times Blade defeated the Guardian, it never stayed down. With time, it would repair itself. He'd done the exact same thing yesterday, and it had come right back.

But at least they'd have peace for a day or so.

○ Scene V: The Next Day, at the Proving Ground

The Guardian was back the next day, sitting atop the same pile of rubble as before, resting her chin on one raised knee as she stared at Blade.

"She's back again," Blade said to his usual sparring partner.

"She sure is," replied Earnest. "But that's fine, isn't it?"

Um, no? Blade had no idea when the girl currently staring at him would decide to start launching artillery fire. So for now, he was sparring with Earnest, dodging and catching her sword, while at the same time keeping an eye on the Guardian. Truth be told, it was pretty draining.

"This is good training for you, too, Blade. Don't you think?" Earnest said with a mischievous grin.

Great. She must've noticed that I'm not giving her my full attention.

Unlike yesterday, the Guardian wasn't making any moves to attack, nor was she smugly boasting about her specs. She was just staring at Blade, holding her knee.

"I wonder if she likes you," Earnest mused.

"What makes you say that?"

"She's staring right at you."

How thick do your rose-colored glasses have to be to imagine that? Earnest might see things that way, but from Blade's viewpoint, the Guardian was staring at him in an attempt to gauge his combat capabilities. With each move Blade made, the Guardian was logging more data on his abilities and quirks.

Not that he was particularly concerned. He'd run into lots of opponents like this during his Hero days. If you had so little experience as a fighter that letting the enemy figure out your moves got you in trouble, you could never be a Hero. Not that Blade was a Hero anymore.

"Do you think she wants to get to know you?" suggested Earnest.

"What makes you say that?"

Now she was just being outrageous. They were talking about a Guardian. Those things were born killers, originally made to serve as berserkers in war.

"You're only saying that because you don't know how dangerous that thing really is," said Blade.

"Wasn't it the same with Cú?"

"Huh?"

"Didn't Cú perch somewhere like that and stare at everyone the same way?"

Blade looked at the Guardian.

It was true. Back when she'd first arrived, Cú had stared at Blade and the others just like the Guardian was now, from the same kind of perch. Her gaze had been full of envy, and yet Blade, her own father, hadn't noticed her feelings. His lack of insight had ended up causing Cú a lot of pain.

"Huh? What? …Wait, you think she wants to join us, too?"

"Well, we don't know that yet, do we?"

"But didn't you just say that? Like, literally just now." Blade pouted, and Earnest chuckled at him.

"Oh, look, Claire's charging in."

Claire was the most compassionate, caring girl in the whole class, and now she was quietly working her way toward the Guardian. Her trepidation was clear, but she maintained a smile as she approached the girl from the side.

Come to think of it, wasn't Claire the one holding the Guardian's hand when it first arrived? Back when it looked like a robot and not a hot girl, that is. Of course, that "hand" was really more of a feeler capable of paralyzing anything it touched, but still.

Once Claire was right up next to her, the Guardian extended a feeler out from her neck and smashed it against the ground. The concrete exploded, leaving deep gouges in the floor. This was a pretty clear intimidation tactic, but Claire didn't falter. As Blade and everyone else knew well, she was a pacifist, but she had guts.

"Hey, there. I'm sure you're bored just watching. Would you like to join us?"

Claire opted for a straight-down-the-middle approach. They were pretty far away from Blade, but he could still hear everything. He had something called "Hero Ears"—a classic Hero-level skill.

"My mission is to terminate my target," replied the Guardian. "I am currently observing him to gather data. You are not targeted for termination, but if you interfere, I will eliminate you."

"Okay, sure. There are lots of girls like that. So how about you join us?"

There are definitely not *lots of girls like that...or are there? The Overlord is always insisting she'll be the one to kill me and so on.*

"Cooperative action is not included in my programming."

I guess that makes sense. Blade had never seen a bunch of Guardians in a pack before—not once in his seventeen years of Hero-dom. If they ever ganged up, even a Hero could wind up in a pickle. He might even have to break out some Hero force. But then, a Hero was supposed to use Hero force when things got serious.

"Well," Claire said, "if it's not, you can start learning now! Yessica and I are good at fighting as a team, you know."

"I do not think it would be of benefit for me to learn how humans fight. I am not a human." The Guardian's expression and voice were as cold as could be. But Claire was invincible when it came to stuff like this.

Still smiling, she looked at the Guardian and said, "Hey, Iona?"

"Iona?"

"The letters on your chest. They say 'IONA,' don't they? Isn't that your name?"

"They do not say 'IONA.' They read '10NA.' Ten-N-A. That is my identification and model number. I do not have a name."

"Oh? Well, if you don't have a name, why don't we just go with Iona?"

See? Invincible. And now the Guardian had a name: Iona.

"Hey, how're they doing? Are they almost done? How's it looking?" Earnest was watching the Guardian, one hand shading her eyes.

"Not sure," said Blade casually.

"Well, I, for one, have never seen a girl that can resist Claire's smile."

Now that Blade thought about it, wasn't the Empress won over by that same smile not too long ago? And now the two of them were great friends.

"So look," said Claire. "If you really want to beat Blade, we've got something called the Super-Being Subjugation Committee."

"Geh." Blade grumbled at this.

"What? What's wrong?" Earnest said. She couldn't hear their conversation.

"Oh, it's nothing..."

Blade didn't have to listen in to know how the Guardian—or rather Iona, would respond to that. She was already clasping Claire's offered hand.

○ Scene VI: The Super-Being Subjugation Committee

"Today, as chairman, I am pleased to welcome a new member to our committee," Leonard declared.

They were in a locked room with the curtains drawn, and Leonard was the only one standing. The rest of them nodded along from their seats in the darkness.

There was no real reason to draw the curtains, or for that matter, to lower the lights to the point where the attendees couldn't make out one another's faces. It was all done simply to create the atmosphere of a secret society. While in a real secret society, members would meet in the dark so as not to expose their identities, everyone in the Super-Being Subjugation Committee already knew everyone else. Originally, the group had simply come together under the united slogan of "Let's beat Blade!"

"Moving on to the first item on our agenda," Earnest said, taking over after the chairman's opening remarks. "Are we gonna call this girl Iona, then?"

"There is no meaning in assigning me an individual name. However, as an artificial intelligence, I see no reason to object to your calling me 'Iona' for the sake of convenience."

"…Sounds like a yes to me," said Earnest.

The Guardian-turned-pretty-girl had a strangely stilted way of speaking. Without Earnest interpreting for her, Blade would have had no idea if she was saying yes or no.

"…So why are *you* here, Blade?" asked Earnest.

"What? Am I breaking some law? I *am* this group's special adviser, you know. What's so weird about me attending meetings?"

"I thought you didn't want to be an adviser."

"That's not how I remember it."

Being the adviser for a group that sought to defeat him wasn't a weird concept for him at all. It was just like back when he apprenticed with that revered old magic beast, and they'd worked together to figure out ways for Blade to defeat him. *See? Totally normal.*

"Well, whatever," Earnest replied.

"You wanted hot chocolate, right, Blade?" said Claire.

"Oh, yeah. Thank you."

Claire was handing out drinks to the attendees. She went around to Leonard, then Earnest, then Sophie and Cú for whatever reason, before finding Eliza from the engineering department. The Overlord was also participating, if only to kill time. "Do not forget—it is *I* who will defeat you" was quickly becoming her catchphrase.

This lineup comprised the core members of the group, but for this meeting, they had four additional attendees—Clay, Kassim, Yessica, and Claire.

After she'd made her rounds, Claire brought some tea over to the robot girl.

"Iona… Um, can you drink tea?"

"Such a task is child's play for someone with my high-spec functionality. Software and hardware to break down organic matter, absorb it, and use it as energy have already been installed."

"Oh."

Blade wondered why she had to talk so much just to say whether or not she could drink tea. And she always rattled off her words at a breakneck pace with that same blank expression. It was jarring to hear such smug language come from a face with such lovely features.

"The individual named Claire said that if I came to this place, there was a high probability that we would find a way to terminate my target, Blade."

"Just 'Claire' is fine."

"Yeah, and you can just call me 'Blade.'"

"Very well. Blade, I will do everything in my power to eliminate you. I have concluded that doing so is the only way to accomplish my mission. Fortunately, your genetic code has not been entered into this country's registry of citizens, so terminating you does not violate the Three Laws. In conclusion, I am fully capable of harming you. My conclusion has been approved, and is currently supported, by Mother."

"Can someone translate?"

"I think she's trying to say, 'I'm angry at you, so let me punch your lights out,'" said Earnest.

"Are you sure?"

"How should I know? I have no idea what she means by 'genetic code,' or 'Three Laws,' or 'registry of citizens.' Eliza, do you know?"

"I have some idea," said Eliza, the most scientifically minded of the group. "But it would take a while to explain. By the way, my brain requires a great quantity of sugar to support its advanced thought processes."

"Oh, I understood that," said Blade. "Eliza wants us to fork over some snacks."

"That much was obvious," said Earnest. "…Here."

She put down a heavy-looking bag of snacks. She always had a ton of them in her dorm room, a fact everyone was always taking advantage of.

Once Claire had finished passing out snacks and tea, she returned to her seat.

"Hey, Iona," she said as she crunched away on a pretzel, "why are you trying to terminate Blade, anyway?"

Earnest had finished her pretzel in a single bite. She was consuming her snacks about ten times as quickly as a normal person. Blade thought it was about time people started categorizing her as nonhuman, too. If he was a super-being, maybe they should call Earnest a "super–black hole."

"Because he has repeatedly invaded the central control room that I guard," Iona explained.

"I had the master key, didn't I?" said Blade.

"The key is not enough. Biometric authentication is also required for entry. If there is no trace of the captain's code within your genes, entry is strictly prohibited."

"What's she talking about?" Earnest turned to Blade.

"Well, there's this place called the Royal Forbidden Library…"

"That room is not a library," interrupted Iona. "Its original purpose was—"

"…and when I've got something to research, for example…"

"His most recent intrusion was eighty-seven days ago."

"Three months…," mumbled Earnest. "Wait, you mean…?"

"Yeah, I was doing research on you."

Back when Earnest was struggling to control Asmodeus, her magic sword, Blade had gone down below the palace to figure out the cause and find a solution. That was where the Royal Forbidden Library was hidden, along with its vast stores of information.

And yes, he'd sent the Guardian flying that time, too.

"Oh… So this is all *my* fault?" said Earnest.

"You look like a little girl with a crush, Anna."

"Sh-shut up, Yessica! Ugh! …Just stop, okay?"

"There were thirteen other previous intrusions," Iona said, interrupting again.

Earnest pouted. "Oh, so it *isn't* my fault."

What's with her? First she seems happy, then she's upset…

"However, I was unable to stop him on any of those thirteen occasions," Iona continued. "I have been destroyed a total of twenty-eight times—"

"Blade! Haven't you destroyed her enough?!"

"Through those twenty-eight destructions, my body has been crushed into a total of 577,526 fragments—"

"Blade! That's too many pieces!"

"And I have endured Mother's scoldings for a grand total of 500,037,000 milliseconds—"

"Your boss yells at you too much!"

Earnest looked miffed, like she was taking this personally. Nobody was better at getting angry than she was. If there were four core emotions to the human psyche—joy, anger, sadness, and fun—everybody knew which one best represented Earnest.

"Wow. So Blade molested you twenty-eight times? That's terrible…" Leonard gently placed a sympathetic hand on Iona's shoulder.

Blade had never met a more melancholy man. Sadness was definitely his defining emotion.

"M-molested?!" shouted Earnest. Her face was bright red. "Leonard! Stop making things weird!"

What does molest *mean again?* Blade was looking around, hoping someone would explain it to him, when he locked eyes first with the blank-faced Sophie, and then with Cú with her great big smile. To continue his earlier line of thought, Cú's defining emotion would be fun, while Sophie's was none of the four—null, maybe?

"Yes," said Iona. "I was shamed an average of 2.15 times per intrusion. And he stays inside for a long time and refuses to leave quickly."

"Ah-ha-ha-ha-ha-ha! This is hilarious! It sounds like you really *did* molest her, Blade!" Yessica was loving this. Her emotion was joy, of course.

"Guys… Please, just stop this… I'm begging you." Claire was bashfully fidgeting in her seat. Her emotion was shame.

"Hey, Overlord, do *you* know what 'molest' means?" Blade decided to ask Ovie, who had a lot of life experience for being just five years old.

"As far as I know, in this context, it means forcibly engaging in sexual mating without the consent of the other person."

"Eugh." Blade groaned.

"Oh, I see," said Iona. "So all I have to do is perform this 'molest' on Blade in return, then?"

"Eugh." He groaned again. "L-look, I know I smashed you up a bunch of times, but… You were still a robot back then, you know?"

"Ah-ha-ha-ha-ha! You're such a monster, Blade!" shouted Yessica.

"Why is that?"

Things were devolving into chaos. But even after everyone had started to calm down, Iona continued to regale her audience with tales of all the "damage" Blade had done to her. That, and how treacherous and depraved Blade was. How abnormal he was—how crazy, even. Quietly, solemnly, she enumerated all her accusations. A lot of it Blade remembered, but some of it was new. All of it was extremely exaggerated.

Everyone nodded at regular intervals. They were entranced. Moved, even.

Blade heaved a big sigh. "Okay, I'm leaving," he told Earnest.

"Sure," she said, not particularly interested.

He looked at Cú and Sophie. Both of them were too wrapped up in Iona's stories to spare him so much as a glance.

After that, he left the room and headed down the hallway.

Well, it's not as bad as I feared, which is a big relief. But that Guardian… Ever since she took human form, she's been acting weirdly…human.

He had attended this meeting of the Super-Being Subjugation Committee because he'd been concerned about something. What if, by some chance, the Guardian lost control and went on a rampage? Blade was about the only one who could subdue her. Even Earnest, Sophie, Cú, and Ovie together probably wouldn't cut it. Her girlish appearance would trick them into thinking they could capture her without destroying her, or something stupid like that. They were doomed to defeat.

Only the Hero, Blade, would be able to smash her into bits with a single blow, quick and merciless, no holding back. *Wait. I'm not a Hero anymore. Scratch that.*

There was no real need to go easy on her in the first place. It wasn't like her body contained a soul. Blade was sure someone like Eliza could explain the details using a lot of difficult ancient vocabulary…but whether a Guardian's body looked like a young girl or a robot berserker, they were nothing more than puppets, controlled remotely by something or someone else. Destroying them wasn't a problem. Nothing of value was lost. No one died, because Guardians had never had a soul. And their bodies would repair themselves anyway, thanks to those nano…nano-somethings. That ancient technology stuff.

Because Blade knew all this, he never hesitated to rip the Guardian apart. If he thought he was killing her… Well, yeah, he might hesitate a little.

Back in his Hero days, he'd never had the luxury to hesitate. But he was a normal person now, so he decided to take all the time he wanted to agonize over the situation.

○ Scene VII: The Conference

Blade might have left, but everyone at the meeting continued to talk about him.

"Using my little gray cells to deduce the truth, I, Eliza Maxwell, believe that was the main reason for your defeat. That's why he showed you no mercy."

"You think so?" Iona said, raising an eyebrow.

She had learned by watching the others at the meeting that this body movement was meant to indicate mild doubt. Each moment, Iona was thinking and growing. For someone as advanced as her, such feats were child's play.

"Oh, definitely," said a girl with red hair. "For sure. That sounds just like Blade."

Based on her observations, Iona deduced that this girl was the central figure in the room. She was also the closest person to Iona's target, Blade.

"You know, he can be weirdly cold at times," the red-haired girl continued. "Scary, even. Like, he told me once that he was gonna cut me up. He was *totally* serious about it, too. If I had lost control, he really would have slashed me to ribbons."

"Bragging about your love again?" asked Eliza, adjusting her glasses.

"Br... *Bragging?!* O-of course not!"

"She talks about him all the time unsolicited," Deemo said. She had taken Eliza's glasses and put them on her own face, and now she was taking a moment to adjust them. "Hee-hee! I've got some stories of my own, though. I once turned down Blade's advances, you know."

"Huh? Whoa... What?! When did he confess?!"

"Huuuuuuuuh?"

Claire yelped. Yessica was laughing, while Sophie remained expressionless. Cú stifled a yawn. The boys all looked uncomfortable as they waited for this wave of girl talk to pass.

Deemo continued. "He said, 'Why don't you just stay at this school for good?' A clear confession of love! And I said, 'No—I'll kill you, then leave so I can find someone stronger!'"

"Oh. So that's what you meant," said Earnest. "The way you phrased it, you had me freaking out for a second. That's just him 'making friends' like he usually does. Besides, Deemo, you've been friends with him for ages now, right? So much for turning him down."

"Ha-ha-ha! You're not wrong." Deemo couldn't help but laugh.

"I will be the one to terminate the individual called Blade," announced Iona.

"Hmm? What's gotten into you all of a sudden?" asked Deemo.

"The intruder Blade is my target. I must use everything in my power to defeat him."

"Mmm. Well, after you, then."

"Yeah. It doesn't matter which of us beats him," said Earnest. "We're just here to see him go down. That's what this committee is all about."

"It is?" Iona raised an eyebrow, displaying her mild doubt once again.

Logically speaking, if Iona killed the individual named Blade—if she stopped his life activity—no one else would be able to kill him afterward. Human logic was something Iona had trouble with.

"I wish to discuss this matter constructively," she continued. "What should I do to defeat him?"

"Okay," said Earnest. "Let's get to it. Now we're finally starting to sound like a real Super-Being Subjugation Committee."

"The way I, Eliza Maxwell, see it, instead of debating how to take out Blade, Iona should think of ways to prevent Blade from defeating her."

"I have thought over the matter, and these are the results," Iona announced.

She threw out her chest, and her thick chest armor jiggled. Her breasts' elasticity and coefficient of restitution were both faithful reproductions of the real thing, as was their internal structure, including the layer of flexible fat and the ligament structures that retained each one's shape. As a result, they shook and trembled exactly the same way as a human girl's.

"So why did you decide to become a girl?"

"According to my observations, the individual called Blade goes easier on female opponents."

"Does he? I'm not so sure…," said Earnest.

"Oh, he absolutely does!"

"Yeah, all the time!"

"Mm-hmm…"

Clay, Kassim, and Leonard all nodded firmly.

"…Okay, maybe he does," said Earnest, increasingly convinced. "So you thought he'd put up less of a fight if you looked like that?"

Iona nodded, indicating her agreement.

"Aww, that's cute!" Earnest jumped on Iona and squeezed her. The latter's expression never changed. "…Oops! Oh, dear, I got carried away…" It took Earnest a few seconds to regain her composure.

"I suppose that strategy failed, though," Eliza remarked.

"Yes. As you said earlier, the cause of my defeat was due to being controlled remotely. I would like to provide additional explanation regarding that point. This body is indeed being controlled from a remote location. The resulting time lag is on the order of nanoseconds, never reaching a microsecond in length. This is most certainly beyond a human's reaction time, and thus should not impair my combat abilities in any way."

"Controlled...remotely?" Earnest blinked.

"About that...," Eliza began.

She provided a brief explanation for everyone in the room, Earnest included. Eliza was the only one present with expertise on the lost technology Iona was describing.

"To put it plainly, it means that her soul is being kept in another location."

"Huh? What?"

"I can't be sure whether she's an advanced AI or if she has achieved full personhood. We don't even know if she exists purely in the form of data, or if her architecture encompasses the physical structure of her core unit as well—"

"I am adaptable to either purpose. My current ego is a seventeen-zettabyte block of data stored in a subunit controlled by Mother. However, it can also be installed in a core unit, around four inches in diameter, that is specially designed for that purpose."

"Four inches? Just about the size of a human heart. I assume it can be built in, yes?"

"Affirmative. However, if installed in a physical core, my personality will be lost if the core is fatally destroyed, regardless of what happens to my body."

"Yes, of course."

"This approach will therefore make me more vulnerable... Do you think it is the correct method?"

"Haven't you already weakened yourself in an attempt to beat him?"

"Yes, I have."

Iona paused to think. She brought a hand to one side of her head and tilted her neck five or so degrees. Based on her observations, this gesture, at precisely this angle, stimulated the greatest protective instinct in her audience.

"Um… Hold up. Can you…uh, explain what's going on for me?" Earnest chose her words carefully, leaving a lot of pauses.

"Oh?" said Eliza. "Are you saying the mighty Empress wasn't able to understand that conversation?"

"…Just explain it," Earnest spat.

Everyone laughed. This, Iona gathered, was the right moment for mirth. She thought she had learned a lot about humans, but there was so much more to analyze.

"…Basically," Eliza began, "since her soul is located externally, away from here, that makes her effectively immortal. Her nanomachines can reconstruct her body—her physical form anyway—over and over again."

"Correct. Even if I am completely disintegrated at the atomic or even the subatomic level, as long as there is mass available for utilization around me, I can be restored."

"You don't have to look so smug about it," said Earnest.

"If Blade is aware of this," Eliza continued, "that would explain his behavior. I think he's so merciless toward Iona precisely because he knows he's not doing her any real harm when he destroys her. For him, it's the same thing as chopping the Empress in half in the virtual world—"

"Don't call me 'the Empress.' And *don't* discuss me being chopped in half."

"Or decapitating Sophie…"

"That was quite a sight, yes," Sophie agreed.

"Or turning Cú into mincemeat…"

"That really hurt!" Cú exclaimed. "It was great! My honored Father is sooo amazing!"

"Hmm. I will need to give my all during the next virtual training," Deemo said, joining in. "Kill or be killed… Hee-hee! Yes, *that* is how demons express their affection."

"…And that," Eliza concluded, "is exactly the type of relentless brutality Blade is demonstrating against Iona in real life."

"Yeah," said Earnest. "Blade can be merciless sometimes, huh? Scary, even… Though I kind of like it."

"Anna. Anna!" exclaimed Yessica. "You're gushing about him again. You're being so obvious."

Everyone laughed. This time, Iona was able to join in.

"Now let's say that Iona wasn't immortal but had a finite lifespan. What then?"

"Like…if she was destroyed…she'd be dead for good?" asked Earnest.

"Yes, exactly. She wouldn't die the same way a human does, but she'd never come back again, and she would be similarly lost forever."

"Then…in that case…I guess Blade wouldn't be able to destroy her."

Eliza pushed her glasses back up her nose. The ceiling light reflected in the lenses, creating a brief flash.

"I think it's worth conducting a few experiments," she said. "I, Eliza Maxwell, hereby christen this project Operation Stand Alone Complex."

○ Scene VIII: The Duel

After school, the Second Proving Ground was filled to capacity. Blade and Iona stood in the middle of the arena, sizing each other up from a distance.

Iona had just warmed up her machinery and was in full battle mode. She was moving her body up and down rhythmically, stepping lightly like a boxer. The air around her shimmered a bit from all the warmth she gave off. Androids like her got physically hot during battle since their bodies couldn't dissipate the excess heat quickly enough. Blade wondered if her long green hair served as a kind of fibrous heat sink.

"I can't believe you haven't gotten sick of having your ass kicked," Blade said, tapping his shoulder with the sword he was carrying.

He had already finished charging up, and six shots were locked and loaded in his body, ready to be fired out in rapid succession. The Proving Ground was pretty spacious, and there were no other girls anywhere near them. This would be a one-on-one battle, so he was free to fire all six shots and blow the Guardian away without mercy.

Seriously, is she ever *gonna give up?*

"Right. Let's do this."

Blade held his sword out in front of him. Lowering his center of gravity, he aimed the tip of his weapon at his target, preparing to launch a hypercharged vortex that would sweep her away and break her down into her component parts.

"Blade, one word before you begin…"

Eliza started to say something, but the match was kind of underway already. Didn't she know that?

"I'd just like to specify that Iona is now working in Stand Alone Mode."

"Huh?" For a moment, he didn't understand. "Stand…Alone…?"

"Yes. Stand Alone. It means…well, 'standalone.'"

"You just said the same thing twice!"

"I'm not sure I can explain it in any simpler terms."

Blade felt like he was being made fun of.

"What she means," Earnest clarified, "is that if you destroy Iona this time, she'll actually die."

"Huh?"

It still made no sense. Iona was a Guardian, after all—immortal by default.

"She'll die, all right? I mean, how can I make this any simpler?"

"N-no, I… I understand what you mean, but… Huh? What?" He turned back toward the android in front of him.

"I can affirm her statement. Currently, the thing equivalent to my soul is housed in a laminate positron crystal inside of my rib cage. I have no current physical connective functionality to Mother. The communication lines have been physically removed, and I am now functioning on a completely independent mobile basis."

"Um… What about your ear things?"

Blade pointed at the earlike appendages on either side of her head. Those were what mechanical-type monsters used to hear the "voice" of whoever was bossing them around. He knew that from his Hero days. Destroying those would disrupt the chain of command, giving him an advantage—but

if they were there, it should mean she was connected to her boss, or Mother, or whoever.

"These? These are for decoration. They are fake transmitters."

"Fake?" Blade mumbled absently.

"My weakness at the moment is right here."

Iona took Blade's hand...and pushed it hard against her chest. Even through her rubber combat suit, he could feel what lay below.

"Inside my chest, within a space of about four inches square, you will find my 'heart.' If it is seriously damaged, the personality that creates me will be permanently lost."

"Stop making him fondle you like that! That is absolutely not necessary!" Earnest was angry. Then again, she was always angry.

"Now that Blade understands the situation, let the battle begin," said Eliza.

Like I said, it's already started.

It was tough for Blade to get used to these staged bouts, where someone had to shout "Begin!" before the battle could commence. In a real fight, there was no starting signal. The moment he detected an enemy in range, whether via sight, presence, or whatever supersensory Heroic skill he had, the battle had already commenced.

"Now... Begin!"

And with that signal, the battle began for everyone else.

o Scene IX: The Bloody Struggle

The fight had already been raging for several minutes.

The combatants were swinging their limbs around with tremendous force. Punches and kicks flew through the air. In her previous form, Iona had relied on her feeler-based abilities and light-rays, but now that she had taken on human form, she had switched to a close-range melee style.

A few things surprised Blade about this. For one, she was pretty strong. Her physical control and fighting skills were on par with Sophie's, and her defenses were on the same level as Cú's. The power of the light-ray cannon in her right hand ranked up there with Earnest in Scion mode, and those tricky feeler attacks from behind her neck reminded him of Yessica at her best. Even when dodged, repelled, or beaten to the ground, she just kept on attacking. In that way, she was as resilient in battle as Claire.

Even more unexpected than all that was the hesitation Blade found within himself. Realizing he could hesitate at all in battle was quite a revelation.

One thought rose in his heart: *Wow, I'm really not a Hero anymore, am I?*

He was a little happy about that, and a little sad as well—but most of all, Blade was starting to get flustered.

This…um, isn't good, is it?

Blade wasn't able to fire even one of his six Dragon Eater shots. They were just a *little* too powerful. Now he regretted not charging up something weaker.

He could've used Dragon Smasher, for example. That was the weakest of the dragon-destroying techniques—more a distraction than anything else—and he probably could've worked up twenty or so for later use. With Iona's defenses, a direct hit from one of those would do little more than blow off a couple of limbs. Dragon-destroying techniques were crafted to break through the steely armor of a dragon, inflicting deep wounds. But while Dragon Smasher was one of their number, it wasn't all *that* lethal.

Dragon Eater, the second-weakest in the series, had enough of a bite to slaughter a younger dragon in a single blow, and Iona's offensive and defensive skills were pretty much equivalent to such a dragon. Getting hit with one of those, in other words, was likely to rub her out for good.

So with *that* off the table…

"Hah! Hah! Hah!"

Iona lowered her hips, then leaned her weight into a triple strike, her face as blank as Sophie's in battle. Her blows struck Blade's stomach, crotch, and throat.

"Geeeh! Ooh! Urgggh!"

"Ah-ha-ha-ha-ha-ha! Did you hear that? He said 'urgh'! A super-being said 'urgh'! He's a super-being, but he's grunting like some wild beast!"

Earnest was enjoying this. Blade really wished she'd stop calling him a super-being over and over, though. Each one hurt almost as much as Iona's punches. He tried to block them with fighting force, but they came crashing right through.

"Good one, Iona! Keep it up!"

Now Earnest was carelessly cheering for his opponent, really egging her on.

"Just as we suspected, it appears the super-being is unable to act," Eliza said. "Even a super-being has his weak points, it seems."

I can hear you, you know. Stop calling me a super-being all the time.

Blade threw his sword down.

"Daaaaah! Come *on!*"

He used one of his charged shots. A completely unfocused Dragon Eater, mostly just a strong gust, shot out from his palm.

The blast sent Iona flying back…but she weathered it, though her feet left skid marks on the ground several feet long. She grinned and then lunged at him.

"Urg! Argh! Hrrrph!"

"*Hrrrph!* You hear that? *Hrrrph!* Oh man…!"

Earnest was enjoying herself again—or rather, she was rolling around on the ground, swinging her legs. Anyone who wanted could see right up her skirt.

Blade used up his remaining five charges. They weren't very focused, though, since he hadn't channeled them through his sword. They generated little more than a hurricane-force wind—capable of tearing clothes, but little else. Iona's battle suit was made of some special material, though, and it stayed together. Blade wasn't in a hurry to see her naked or anything… but why were all the boys in the crowd booing? He ignored them with all his might.

"Ergh! Oof! Hrgggh!"

He took a hard strike to the stomach and doubled over. Then Iona used both hands to pound him like a hammer. Cracks formed along the Proving Ground's floor in the shape of a spiderweb.

Man, that hurt. I'm gonna have a lump on my head for sure.

"Hey!" Blade said from the ground, little bits of concrete falling off his forehead. "Take it easy on me!"

"No, Blade. You are the one who will go easy on *me*. It is obvious to me by now that you are incapable of exercising violence against a sweet young girl."

The fight had grown increasingly lopsided. Blade was cornered, his back up against the fence near where Earnest and the others were booing him. He had no more space to retreat.

"You are unable to attack me. If you tear me apart, the possibility of my physical core being destroyed is over seventy percent."

Yeah, that sounded about right. That was why he couldn't touch her.

"Your overabundance of offensive force is the reason you will lose."

But that wasn't the only reason. If he'd had even a little time to knead his spirit, he could have used a less powerful skill or two...but Iona's close-range fighting technique wouldn't allow for that. He'd tried to use Dragon Eater just to distance her for long enough to get out some other skill, but it simply wasn't enough.

"Now surrender," she said, cracking her knuckles as she approached. Even that gesture was strangely human. "Or would you like to be made to say 'Hrrrph!' and 'Urgh!' again?"

Blade didn't like the sound of that. He didn't want any more bumps on his head. So he made a decision.

"Okay. I give up. I lose."

"Say it one more time, please," said Iona. "Clearly, so everyone can hear you."

"I lose!"

A loud cheer erupted. The entire audience was on Iona's side, it seemed. Cú and Sophie were probably the only exceptions.

Blade slowly slid down the fence he was leaning against. Looking up at the ceiling of the Proving Ground, Blade suddenly realized something truly amazing. He didn't mind losing at all.

At long last, he was a normal person, not a Hero. Losing didn't mean anything to him. It wasn't like the human race was going to go extinct or anything. He was normal. *This is great!*

Earnest peeked out from above the fence.

"Hey, good match," she said. "You have a big bump on your head. Let me take a look."

Her red silhouette was carrying a first aid kit, and she was smiling.

○ Scene X: Class as Usual

The students were gathered on the same training ground as always, attending class as usual. Time crawled by as it did every day, and everyone was anxiously waiting to fill their plates as soon as the lunch bell rang.

"Hey... Hasn't she seemed pretty down lately?" said Earnest.

"Yeah, I guess so," Blade said as he swung his sword this way and that, parrying her strikes.

Clang, clang.

"I wonder why. I mean, she won."

"Yeah. She sure did."

Blade gave only the laziest of replies. His focus was on their sparring. Each of Earnest's strikes had a certain snappiness to it that defied description. If he failed to address each one properly, he might get hit and cleaved in two. That was how much force was behind them.

"Well, aren't you concerned?"

At that point, she unleashed her most powerful strike yet, sending tendrils of flame into the air. Earnest was getting serious—it'd take more than your garden-variety barrier to block that slash. Blade caught it with his sword. It bit about halfway into the metal, but he stopped it. Asmodeus, on the other hand, wasn't nicked in the least.

Wow. This is working pretty well, huh?

Blade was pleased. Earnest rarely put her full power behind a slash like this, and he made the most of the opportunity.

He had recently started to explore other fighting styles, besides just relying on brute force. In theory, it was possible to completely kill the momentum of a sword if you could catch it with a soft enough hand. If he had to score his block just now, he'd give it at least a five out of ten.

Back in his Hero days, he'd met all kinds of amazing people. Once, he'd seen a withered old man—nothing more than skin and bones—who could stop a full-powered Hero's sword strike with just his fingertips.

"You're pretty cold, aren't you, Blade?"

"Huh? No I'm not," he hurriedly replied. "I'm plenty worried."

"I don't need your lip service," Earnest shot back.

She was right. To tell the truth, Blade wasn't all that concerned.

At last, he turned to face the subject of their conversation.

Iona was perched atop the fence, idly watching their training. She'd finally achieved her long-term goal of defeating Blade. But once she was done, it seemed she'd suddenly lost all her motivation. She just sat there all day long, watching from afar. During practical training, she'd go to the Proving Ground; during lectures, she'd be right outside the classroom window.

What the heck is she doing...?

Even on rainy days, she'd still sit there, not even holding an umbrella. Blade assumed androids didn't catch colds, but still.

"She's a girl, Blade. And you're not the slightest bit worried about her? That's not the Blade I know. You're failing to be Blade."

"But she's *not* a girl. And how am I failing? What did I fail at?"

"*You* were the one going on about making a hundred friends, weren't you? But you won't make friends with her just because she's not human? That's totally out of character."

"Don't be ridiculous." Blade grimaced. What was she implying?

"I mean, Cú's a dragon—a magical creature. Deemo's a half-magic beast. Ein and Zwei are spirit birds. You've had a pretty open mind about who you befriend for most of your time here, haven't you?"

Now that he thought about it, she kind of had a point.

"Heeey!" Blade yelled across the training ground, waving his sword. "Wanna come over here and join us?!"

Iona turned toward him...but then shook her head once, climbed down off the fence, and walked away.

"What the heck is she up to?" Blade wondered aloud.

○ Scene XI: The Dining Hall at Lunch

Blade was late to the dining hall for lunch, and nearly every seat had been taken. Squeezing his hand around his companion's to make sure she didn't get lost, he searched for somewhere the two of them could sit.

"Hey, Blade, why're you so late?"

It was Clay who called out to him first from their usual lunch table. But the moment he looked at Blade, he froze up, confused.

Well, now that we've been seen, there's no more reason to hide...

Blade headed for his usual seat.

"Wait," Yessica said, "you brought Iona along with you?"

"Yeah. I went and grabbed her."

"You're holding hands!" This was apparently devastating news to Earnest.

Didn't he just say he'd grabbed her? Of course he had her by the hand. What was the big deal?

"Please let me go," said Iona. "Eating food is not a requirement for my kind."

"You haven't taken in any electricity, either, have you?"

Blade had Iona sit down. The table was over capacity, but the people at the neighboring one scooted down to free up a seat.

"I still have sufficient energy stores remaining. If I merely sit and observe, I can remain operational for two hundred years before refueling."

"He was holding her hand!" Earnest shouted.

"Can you shut up?" said Blade.

"He told me to shut up!"

"Hey, can you talk to the king and have him work everything out? Like, the school admission procedures and all that? I know there's a bunch of stuff you have to do."

Obviously, Iona was going to be admitted as a student. Even the Overlord's daughter was attending classes like nothing had happened, so why not have a Guardian or two straight from the underground labyrinth (in cute girl form, of course)? It wasn't like the sky was going to start falling.

"Hey, Iona," said Blade. "Everyone's been talking about how you're acting weird these days."

"Could it be burnout, perhaps?" suggested Eliza. "And by that, I mean the phenomenon of having achieved a goal, then suddenly becoming less motivated in general. I'd be rather interested to see if human psychology could be applied to an android AI."

While Eliza clearly had an academic interest in the topic, she seemed worried, too, in her own way…or so Blade thought, at least.

"Blade," Iona said, "are you concerned about my wellbeing?"

"Nah, not really."

Why should he be? He'd only brought her here because Earnest insisted.

"He said he's worried," said Earnest.

"Stop translating for me."

"I am not sure what is meant by 'burnout,' but…perhaps I *have* experienced a sense of loss after achieving my goal." Iona was finally being honest. "The super-being seemed like such a menacing opponent…but now that I have defeated him, I wonder if this is all there was to it."

"Whoa there," said Blade.

"I went to the trouble of creating this cute human female form, but now I am not sure it was worth such an effort."

"Hey now."

You can't just go around humble bragging like that.

"You wanna take this outside? I can beat you up again for old time's sake."

"Ah-ha-ha-ha-ha!" Yessica was laughing it up. "Oh no, Blade's all riled up! He's totally pissed off! He's acting just like all the other guys!"

"All the other guys"—specifically Clay, Kassim, and Leonard—seemed uncomfortable with her appraisal.

"My goal has been accomplished. A single win is sufficient. It does not matter how that win was achieved. Simply having won comes as a great relief. All my resentment has left me. I no longer remember the approximately twenty-eight times I was destroyed, nor the 577,526 individual pieces I was disintegrated into."

"It sure *sounds* like you remember. You haven't forgotten the numbers, and you keep saying them out loud."

"I have also learned the human art of deceptive criticism. You purposely state the opposite of what is true. Eliza makes use of it often."

"Who, me?" asked Eliza.

"Here you go, Blade, one extra-large katsu curry," said Claire. "Is the same all right for you, Iona?" She had just returned from fetching lunch for the two of them.

"Thank you very much. I still have energy remaining, but I will stay replenished via the digestion and absorption of these organic substances."

Despite what she said, Iona simply gazed at the katsu curry in front of her.

"Do you not know how to eat it?" asked Blade.

"I do."

"Then do you not like spicy food or something?"

"I am a high-spec machine with a built-in taste sensor. However, this sensor provides only data. Therefore, the taste of an organic substance cannot interfere with or block my ability to ingest it."

If she was okay with spice, she could have just said so. All the rest of that stuff was totally unnecessary. Blade glanced at Sophie. She and Iona resembled each other a little, he felt. At least in terms of their expressions and manner of speaking.

"But should I run into an issue impossible to solve through my own capabilities, would you recommend I consult with others about it?"

Blade's first thought was *Ahh, I knew it.* Iona's problem wasn't burnout, as Eliza had suggested. She was having issues of a slightly different nature.

"What's up, Iona? Is something troubling you?"

Earnest was being surprisingly kind to her. She wasn't angry *all* the time. Sometimes she could be really nice to people. As long as they weren't Blade, that is.

"It seems that my architecture has a built-in condition that requires the presence of a higher authority."

"...What now?"

This made no sense to anyone. The entire table turned to Eliza.

"So you need some higher existence to function properly?" she asked.

Iona nodded.

Come on, Eliza. You have to break it down more, or what's the point of translating?

"Yes. When I had a problem I could not solve with my own abilities, I would request a solution from Mother. Then, when I completed Mother's orders, I would report back to her and receive the next mission. Without Mother or a substitute authority, I feel terribly uneasy."

"Who is this Mother person?" Blade asked. The word kept popping up, and he couldn't continue ignoring it.

"Isn't it obvious? She's referring, of course, to the Mother Computer." Eliza frowned at the table as if to say, "You didn't even know that?"

"Hmm… So, Iona. It sounds like you're struggling with your own Stand Alone Complex. I only intended it as the name of this operation—and a clever one, too, if I may say so myself—but now it's become your reality, hasn't it?"

"The name of *what* operation?" asked Blade.

"Shut up," said Earnest.

Blade did as she commanded and quieted down. *Hmph.*

"But if being offline and away from Mother is the issue, why don't you just reconnect?" asked Eliza. "Isn't it just a matter of switching out of Stand Alone Mode and going back online?"

"I have restored my communication functions…but all queries to Mother are currently being rejected."

"Why is that?"

"Dereliction of duty. One-sided closing of the connection. For these and other reasons, my device registration has been terminated. It appears I have been deemed a defective product."

"Well, crap…" Earnest looked up at the ceiling.

"You understood all that?" asked Blade.

"It's like getting fired from school, right? Getting expelled, I mean."

Ohhh. That is *pretty rough.*

"What were the 'other reasons'?" asked Eliza.

"I sent Mother approximately fifteen terabytes' worth of abusive language."

"That's probably the main reason, don't you think?"

"Oh, what's wrong with yelling at someone?" said Earnest. "I mean, I have a *lot* I want to say to the king. Fifteen sheets of writing paper aren't nearly enough."

"Aren't you supposed to call him Your Majesty?" asked Blade. "Aren't you being disrespectful?"

"Screw that."

"Was that directed at me or the king?"

"Oh, I'd never say that to him. That'd be disrespectful."

"Okay," Eliza said, cutting in. "So you just need a higher authority, right?"

Iona nodded.

"Well, then why don't we go with *him*?"

"Whoa, don't even say it. Don't suggest the king. *Anyone* but him. Just not that guy."

"I wasn't planning to…but it sounds like the person in question is already in agreement. Would you be all right with that, Iona?"

"Him? He fulfills the logical conditions, yes. A 'higher authority' is defined in my installed architecture as a person or thing with the ability to surpass me."

"Wait. Who are you suggesting?" asked Blade.

"The human individual referred to in this circle as a 'super-being,'" Iona replied.

"Wait, *me*?!"

Blade was shocked. It had all sounded like someone else's problem. He'd never imagined they were talking about *him*. He was happy to have been referred to as a "human," at least.

"S-so you want me to be this higher authority or whatever?"

Iona took Blade's hand and gazed up into his eyes.

"May I call you…Master?"

"No," he said immediately, refusing her.

"Why not?" asked Earnest. "Look at that poor girl! How does being her master hurt you?"

"This whole thing started with her saying she wanted to terminate me."

"But I never did terminate you. Did I, Master?"

"Stop calling me 'Master.' Please."

"Your refusal troubles me. If you do not become my master, the countdown will continue."

"Huh? What countdown?"

"In order to prevent ourselves from eventually going berserk, Guardians who fall outside the chain of command initiate a self-destruct sequence. This is the countdown I am referring to."

"Huh? Self-destruct?"

"Yes. Self-destruct."

"Um, what?"

It took a few seconds for the meaning behind that word to fully penetrate Blade's mind.

"Whaaaaat?! Self-destruct?!"

Most people within earshot of the conversation leaped to their feet, their chairs clattering. There were a few stragglers, however, making it abundantly clear who had been paying attention. Within audible range, the only people remaining in their seats were a blank-faced Sophie, an absently yawning Cú, and Ovie, gobs of whipped cream around her mouth as she devoured a post-lunch dessert.

"Wait, self-*destruct?* When, *when*?!" Earnest grabbed Iona by the shoulders and shook her hard.

"There is no need for concern," the robot girl replied, her head bobbing from side to side. "When the time comes, I intend to move to a deserted location to carry out the self-destruct sequence."

"That's not the issue!" shouted Earnest. "When is that going to be?!"

A number gradually became visible on Iona's forehead. It was six digits long, and it decreased by one every second.

"Huh? A number? Is that the countdown? Um, three hundred thousand... How much is this?"

"303,752 seconds," Eliza said after a quick glance. "...That's a little over eighty-four hours. Three and a half days."

"*Whaaaaaaaat?!*"

"Blade! Blade!" shouted Earnest. "Come on, Blade, say something! Say something!"

"So she's gonna self-destruct in a few days, huh? Sounds rough."

"That's all you have to say?!"

"Calm down. Don't make a fuss. Can't you be a little more like Sophie and them?"

Sophie stared blankly. Cú let out another yawn. The Overlord was perfectly calm, as if even the end of the world was no concern of hers.

"I think this more than merits making a fuss!"

"But hmm... I see. So the berserkers that sometimes attack are what happens to you guys at the end of your lives? I guess they're kind of like stray Guardians."

"Such units have become so warped that their self-destruct mechanism no longer functions," Iona replied. "I am a high-spec machine functioning normally, however, so my mechanism is still fully operational."

"I dunno about that. If you were 'functioning normally,' I don't think you'd be rebelling against this 'Mother' person. And you wouldn't have been trying to get back at me for destroying you, either."

"Doing so brought me great relief."

"Also, *normal* Guardians don't, you know, turn into girls."

"I am cute, am I not?" She flashed him a smug smile.

Normally, her expression remained blank. But every so often, she'd shoot you a smile that made your heart skip a beat.

Blade responded with a deep, audible sigh.

"So if I become your 'master' or whatever, that'll stop you from self-destructing?"

"Yes, probably."

Another sigh.

"All right... I'll do it."

○ Scene XII: The Now-Familiar Breakfast Routine

Earnest's gang was having their usual breakfast, at the same dining hall as always.

"*Yawwwwwwn…*"

A massive yawn escaped Blade's mouth. Cú, on his lap, followed his lead and let out her own, which was just as impressive.

"That was a very big yawn, Master," said Iona.

She had just returned to the table, carrying meals for both Blade and his dragon daughter. For Cú, she provided a colorful, well-balanced spread. For Blade, a large katsu curry.

Several days had passed since Iona began calling Blade "Master," and the "countdown" to self-destruction or whatever seemed to have stopped. Three and a half days had long passed, and nothing had happened.

Iona hadn't yet been officially enrolled, but she had already been fully accepted as part of the academy. Ein and Zwei the spirit birds were welcomed as friends, and even the Overlord's daughter had been allowed to attend. Iona, who was in human form from the start, had adjusted to school life in record time.

Blade, on the other hand, hadn't been sleeping well lately. Iona wouldn't let him rest at night—not because of any "desire to mate" as the school's doctor was always talking about, but for other reasons.

During the night, Iona would kneel in a corner of Blade's room—perfectly still, her eyes wide open, even in total darkness. She'd stay there the whole time, staring at Blade, never blinking.

If it was just that, Blade would have been fine. The problem was that once Blade entered the deeper stages of sleep, she'd occasionally shower him with murderous vibes. Was she out to kill him in his sleep or something? Blade wasn't sure. Iona herself framed the activity a little differently, calling it "reconfirming that my master is a higher authority." Nevertheless, every time it happened, Blade would automatically wake up. Couldn't she understand that?

But…maybe Blade *was* getting a little soft. He didn't recall ever having a restful night's sleep in his Hero days. In the middle of the battlefield, maybe he could get away with losing consciousness for a few minutes at a time, but he never sheathed his sword. That was pretty much all the sleep a Hero got. If he was at the point of complaining about not getting a full night's rest, wasn't that proof he'd gotten used to living the high life? *Being a normal person is so awesome! I love all this peace and relaxation!*

"By the way…," he said.

"Yes, Master? Do you have an order for me?"

"Not an order, no…but what's with your outfit?"

Blade was looking right at her as he spoke, all the while stuffing Cú's breakfast of bread and scrambled eggs into her mouth.

"You mean this?"

Iona made her black dress and white apron flutter. She wasn't wearing her usual battle suit today.

"This is the ancient garb of a servant. I found it in the archives. Does it not please you?"

Flutter.

"Can you stop fluttering your skirt around like that? It makes all the guys here scrunch up their faces."

Clay, Kassim, and Leonard all hurried to regain their composure.

"If you are ordering me to stop, I will do so immediately."

"While we're at it, can you stop staring at me?"

She was currently sitting across from him watching his every move, never blinking. It made it fiendishly difficult to digest.

"If that is an order…"

"It's not an order or anything, okay? …Fine. Just keep doing it."

"Understood. That's an order, yes? I will proceed to refrain from refraining."

Iona began happily uttering nonsense. Blade let out a deep, deep sigh and waited patiently for the petulant Cú to open her mouth so he could shovel in some salad.

"What're you sighing for, Blade?" asked Earnest.

"Oh, I don't know… It's just…I feel like I've lost something."

"What?"

"...My freedom, maybe?"

Blade shook his head. Having someone call you "Master," snuggle up to you and devote themselves to taking care of you might sound nice, but in reality it was anything but. Blade felt like Iona was the one in control, and he was being made to go along with *her* whims.

"What do you mean?"

"If you don't understand, forget it."

"Hee-hee! ...Earnest, you'd make an excellent first wife," said the Overlord. "So magnanimous! So tolerant! You've really got what it takes."

"You—stop being so *stupid*! It's way too early in the morning for such nonsense, Deemo!"

"Oh, come now. It's fine."

"No, it's not," blurted out Sophie. She was quiet enough that a normal person might not have heard her...but with his Hero Ears, Blade picked up on it. Of course, he wasn't a Hero anymore...

"What's wrong, Sophie?" Blade asked. But Sophie simply spooned more soup into her mouth, mechanically emptying her bowl. He began to wonder if he'd simply imagined her comment.

"If you want to say something, just say it, okay?"

"Is that an order?" Sophie stared straight at him, deadly serious.

Blade pondered for a bit, then nodded. "...Yes it is."

Sophie had a habit of asking "Is that an order?" in response to everything. She'd long struggled with spontaneous behavior. Blade hated to take advantage of that, but if he didn't, he knew Sophie would never speak her mind.

"That's not fair, Master," said Iona. "You never give me any orders. You only give them to Ms. Sophie."

"Keep quiet."

"Ooh, an order! ♪"

A blue vein popped up on Sophie's temple. "I...am unhappy."

"Unhappy with what?" Blade asked.

It was unheard of for Sophie to express dissatisfaction over anything. Even if the dining hall offered the same menu every day for a week, she never complained. That was just who she was. Now everyone at the table was listening, nervously wondering what would happen next.

"She's stolen my bit."

"What?"

"She's stolen my bit."

"Huh?"

"First, she's just as expressionless as I am."

"I am not expressionless," protested Iona. "I have one hundred and eight different facial expressions installed. My camouflage is perfect."

Iona's blank look as she spoke did little to back up what she was saying. She might be able to make any number of faces, but she wasn't using any of them. And had she just called it "camouflage"?

"Second, we both require orders to do anything."

"Um…," the android began.

It was unusual for Sophie to assert herself so clearly.

"I am afraid I cannot help that," Iona continued. "For an android, waiting for orders is instinctual. If an android did not accept commands, it would be considered defective." She was on the counterattack. *Didn't she do just that pretty recently, though?*

"Blade always tells me, 'I don't have any orders for you. Just do what you want,'" said Sophie. "But here he is, giving you orders. That's unfair."

"Huh? What?" Blade was confused.

He looked at Sophie, then Iona. They were now talking directly to each other, ignoring him.

"It's a real war zone in here, huh?" Leonard patted him on the shoulder. "And as a master of this kinda thing, a word of advice. In this situation, you can't take either girl's side. No defending or advocating for either one. Am I clear?"

"Um, okay…"

Blade had no idea what was going on, but he nodded anyway. The handsome Leonard certainly seemed like a veteran of guy-girl "war zones."

"Good luck, then. I'll be praying for you."

Praying?

First period was about to start, and everyone was heading off to their classrooms. All except for Sophie and Iona, who were still in the dining hall, glaring at each other. With no idea what to do, Blade stayed seated, even after the bell rang.

○ Scene XIII: A Tense Lunch Break

Morning lectures passed by peacefully enough. But when lunch break arrived, it was back to the war zone.

"Your large katsu curry, Master," said Iona.

"Th-thanks."

Katsu curry *was* his favorite, but not even *he* ate it every single day for every single meal. Iona must have recorded a database entry somewhere reading "Blade's Favorite: Katsu Curry" or something.

"Hey, uh, by the way, Sophie…what…are you wearing?" he asked.

"Meow."

"Um, that…doesn't answer my question…"

"Meow," repeated Sophie.

She bent her wrists forward and held them in the air while facing Blade. On her head were two triangles that looked like cat ears. A bushy tail was hanging from her rear end. Was she trying to imitate a cat?

"That looks good on you, Sophie," said Earnest. "I was wondering why you wanted to borrow party accessories. Come on, Blade, can't you at least compliment her?"

Blade looked at Earnest, surprised. "Huh? Is that what she wants?"

"Meow."

"Um, Sophie… Enough with the meowing, okay? I'm gonna need you to explain in humanspeak."

"I'm working on a new bit," she said, relenting. "Is it not working?"

"A new bit?"

"Yes. This will help differentiate Iona and me, don't you think?"

"Well, um, I didn't really have trouble telling you apart as you were. Why go through all this effort? You don't have to, um, come up with a new 'bit,' or anything…"

"I don't need your sympathy."

"Umm…" It seemed Sophie had developed some weird hang-ups. How in the world was he supposed to get through to her? "I really don't think this is something you need to worry about…"

"Is that an order?"

"No, like…"

"Master, your orders, please," Iona joined in.

"Uggghh," Blade groaned.

"Hee-hee-hee. Why're you so worked up, Blade?" asked Earnest. "You're acting super weird." She was laughing at him like she didn't have a care in the world.

"You're just laughing 'cause you think this isn't your problem."

"She's totally unconcerned. True first-wife material."

"Stop it, Deemo!"

The Overlord then turned to the others. "Sophie. Iona. If you're that upset with each other, you should decide things with a duel."

"A duel?"

"Yes! The winner can call herself the original, and the loser will be the fake."

"Whoa, don't egg them on!" shouted Blade.

"That's a great idea," said Sophie.

"See? Now you've done it!"

"Very well," Iona agreed. "No matter the contest, I will never lose to a mere human. I am a high-spec machine."

"Don't stop me, Blade," Sophie said.

"Please do not stop me, Master."

"Is that an order?" asked Blade sarcastically. Sighing, he recalled how quick Sophie was to lose her temper. She'd even challenged Blade to an all-out fight once. "I'm fine with you guys duking it out, but keep things peaceful. I'm trying to eat here."

"Give me an example of a peaceful duel," said Sophie.

"Please define 'peaceful,'" chimed in Iona.

Their requests were very similar. *Huh. Maybe they are a lot alike.*

"I dunno," said Blade. "Have a staring contest or something."

Cú and Yessica happened to be in the middle of a staring contest at that very moment. Seeing them had given Blade his inspiration.

"All right."

"I accept."

They faced each other—and then all expression faded from their faces. They looked like mirror reflections. This blank-faced staring contest continued throughout the lunch break. By the time the bell rang, Blade had gobbled down three extra plates of katsu curry.

After that, Sophie and Iona competed at anything and everything.

After their expressionless staring contest ended in a draw, they used their afternoon field training to stage an impromptu Rosewood Academy Championship Match, pitting the artificial Hero against the light-ray-blasting android. In the end, Blade, who was serving as referee, had to conk them both on the head. The match ended in a draw after both sides broke the rules.

In the evening—when most of the students went to the thermae—they competed to see who was better at washing Blade's back. Blade couldn't really tell the difference, so that ended in a draw as well.

It turned out that Iona's green-and-white battle suit was removable, but apart from that piece of trivia, nothing of value came out of the contest.

And so Iona and Sophie stubbornly continued their fight all across Rosewood Academy. Before long, the contests became one of the school's must-see events.

○ Scene XIV: In the Darkness

"Don't worry about it, Blade. Just get some sleep."

"Um…"

"Yes, Master. Please enjoy your rest."

"Now, see here—"

"Yeah, Blade, just get to sleep already."

"Why are *you* here, too?"

A blue, a green, and a red figure were politely kneeling by the wall of Blade's room, watching over him.

"I… Well, I was worried, all right?" said Earnest. "I mean, Sophie and Iona are spending the whole night in your bedroom, so…"

"I don't know what you're worried about, but it's nothing like that, okay? I'll be fine."

Tonight's contest was over who could do a better job of watching over Blade while he slept. Sophie and Iona's competition had already progressed to a new level of nonsense.

"Honored Father, I'm tired!"

"Yeah, okay…"

Cú was rubbing her eyes. She had trouble falling asleep unless Blade covered her up with a blanket, then lightly patted her on the back. That was just how she was.

"All right, I'm turning off the light," said Blade.

It seemed like getting a good night's sleep would be difficult… But he could probably get a few winks in at least.

○ Scene XV: Iona and Sophie

The rhythmic breathing of two sleeping people could be heard in the room. Earnest, leaning against the wall, had completely lost consciousness and was now drooling from the corner of her mouth.

Sophie's and Iona's eyes were wide open, however. There was almost no light in the room, but that didn't bother them. They kept watching Blade's face as he fitfully slept.

"If you are sleepy, you may lie down, Ms. Sophie," said Iona.

"I've been working on my sleep-resistance training. I can stay awake for up to seven days."

"I have no need for sleep in the first place."

"I know."

"I am not sure this battle will reach a conclusion tonight."

"I agree."

"To be honest…lately, I am beginning to wish that our competition would never end."

"……"

Sophie fell silent as Iona continued.

"Before, I was always alone. So much time passed without anyone to spend it with."

Sophie didn't respond. Seconds passed, then minutes. Then at last, she spoke.

"I…am alone, too."

"It wasn't as though I was waiting for him," said Iona, taking Sophie's reply as a cue to continue. "But amid that long, long stretch, he was the only one who came to visit me. He would blow me away and destroy me each time, but—"

"Blade wasn't visiting *you*."

"And you aren't his mother, are you?" Iona met Sophie's jab with her own.

"I… I was alone for so long," Sophie said. "All alone, inside a cage in the corner of a dark laboratory."

Sitting there with the lights off, she stared off into the distance.

"I was nobody. All I had was my value as his copy. He was my only connection to this world." Sophie remained quiet for a while. Then, after what seemed like an eternity, she said, "That's what I thought anyway."

"…Yes," Iona replied. "I was the same. And now you have become someone special to me, too. I am not sure what to do."

"Neither am I."

"I suppose not."

"When I compete with you," said Sophie, "I get this feeling… Could I be having 'fun,' perhaps?"

"I'm not sure I have an answer, Ms. Sophie. You are still a fair bit more human than I am."

"Just Sophie is fine."

"Pardon?"

"Just Sophie is fine. No 'Ms.' is necessary."

"Understood."

And with that, they shut their mouths for the rest of the night, keeping up their unblinking vigil over the lightly napping Blade.

○ Scene XVI: At Breakfast

"Good morning, Master."

"Uhhh…"

They were at the dining hall having breakfast. Iona brought over everyone's food, using both her hands and her feelers—very dexterous of her.

So this is it, huh? The usual routine again…

Blade sighed. Lately it had been day after day of Sophie and Iona quarrelling, their faces devoid of all emotion, pushing him around from dawn until dusk.

Iona served Cú a well-balanced breakfast and Blade a plate of katsu curry. He wished she would update her database entry on him. The curry here was great and all, but he didn't need to eat it for every meal.

"Your breakfast, Sophie."

"Thank you."

Iona put a plate in front of Sophie as well.

"Oh?" Blade did a double take and stared at her.

Wait. Weren't they fighting?

Iona sat down across from Sophie. Her plate was identical to the other girl's—a virtual mirror image.

Um… What?

Blade alone watched the two of them, thoroughly confused.

○ Scene XVII: During Lectures, Too

Iona and Sophie sat next to each other during the morning lectures as well. Iona didn't have any textbooks yet, so Sophie placed hers between them.

"Hey… They're really getting along, huh?" whispered Blade.

"Yeah," Earnest whispered back. "Maybe they're friends now?"

"Why would they be friends?"

"They were both whispering to each other all night. Maybe that's why."

Earnest had participated in the previous night's vigil.

"Yeah, but just talking isn't enough to suddenly make them friends, right? I'd get it if they deepened their bond through a fistfight, but *talking?*"

"If you ask me, becoming friends through punching each other makes a lot less sense. But what does it matter? If they've started getting along, that's great."

"I guess so."

"...Oh! I get it." Earnest smiled ominously. "You feel like she's taken Sophie away from you, right? That's so small-minded."

"Of course I don't!"

"Then maybe you see it as Sophie taking away Iona? Still small-minded."

"Quit it. My mind is *huge!*"

Something about being called "small" subtly hurt him, so Blade vehemently denied Earnest's accusations.

Later, during afternoon field training, Iona teamed up with Sophie, and together they pushed the limits of melee combat. Then there was dinner, and then the open-air bath...

Blade set his eyes squarely on Iona. He made sure to keep her constantly in sight.

"According to my analysis, the main benefit of a warm bath is to promote good blood circulation," she said. "Since I, too, have organic tissue, I have concluded that bathing benefits me beyond simply cleansing my body."

"Hee-hee. Iona, all you have to say at times like this is, 'Mmm, the water feels so good,' okay?" Earnest stretched out in the bath as she spoke.

"Do you feel good, too, Sophie?" asked Iona.

"I've never thought about it before...but, yes, the warm water does feel nice."

"Then it feels nice for me as well."

"Hee-hee. You're all about Sophie, aren't you?"

Earnest was smiling. And Blade—well, the only thought on his mind was how he wanted this scene to last forever. He really did.

Suddenly, he turned to Iona and said, "Let me see the number."

"What was that, Master?" Iona asked, seeming a little confused.

After looking at her quietly for a moment, he said, "The number on your forehead. The countdown... Show me that number again."

"What are you after, Blade?" said Earnest, looking just as confused. "The number? The countdown? Didn't that stop already?"

"Is that an order, Master?" asked Iona.

"That's an order," he said.

The fact that she'd gone to the trouble to ask if what Blade had said was an order confirmed his suspicions.

He had been watching Iona closely all day. He hadn't noticed it back when she was going at it with Sophie, but something about how she behaved now reminded Blade of how the android used to act.

It was a long time ago at this point—back before they were friends, just after she had shown up seeking revenge. After defeating Blade, she'd sat there alone, as if in a daze, staring at everyone else as they trained. Now, just as she had then, she seemed lonely—like she was trying to burn everyone's image into her memory with every second she had left.

She had told them that the countdown had stopped. But nobody had actually checked.

A number lit up on her forehead.

"Huh?!" Earnest exclaimed. "Wait a minute! Seven thousand...?! What's going on?!"

The number was a little over 7,000. It used to be over 300,000.

"It's still going down," said Blade. "So it never stopped?"

"It may not have stopped, but it has slowed down considerably," explained Iona. "The countdown is advancing at a tenth of its initial speed."

"Can someone call Eliza over here?" Blade said.

Not long after, Eliza arrived, rubbing her eyes. Her hair was full of shampoo lather and appeared bright white.

"H-hey! I was in the middle of washing my hair!"

Blade grabbed her head and plunged it into the water, dissipating all the foam.

"Look at this," he said.

Eliza didn't have her glasses on, so she had to get within kissing distance of Iona to see.

"Oh... So it *is* still going, huh?"

"You knew?"

"I *did* think it was pushing it a little having a human be her new master. I thought maybe if that human was a super-being like you, it could work. But I guess super-beings aren't so super after all, huh?"

"But if there's seven thousand left..."

"Assuming the countdown is still proceeding at one tenth of its normal rate, that'd be around twenty hours."

"I see." Blade nodded.

Then he turned to look at Iona. Why hadn't she told him? He decided not to ask her. She, too, must have been torn over whether to say something.

"What do *you* want to do?" he asked.

"I want to watch all of you, for as long as I can, until my final moment. When the time comes, I will go somewhere without any people and self-destruct. It is not my intention to cause any damage to my surroundings."

She said all this casually, as if it meant nothing at all.

○ Scene XVIII: The Farewell Party

"Hold that side up. Yeah. Right there. Now keep it in place."

Everyone was working together to decorate. A garland stretched from one end of the space to the other, and the whole area was festooned with paper balls and stars. There were flowers on the table. They had chosen a spot in the middle of the Second Proving Ground, and all the students were pitching in to freshen it up. There were people from all different cultures, and they were each decorating in their own way, making for a rather chaotic scene.

"That's not food, Cú," said Claire.

"But if I can eat it, doesn't that make it food?"

Claire was putting up strings of cookies shaped like little people, and Cú was grabbing them and gobbling them up. Apparently, the tradition in Claire's homeland was to use sweets as decorations, and even if you weren't Cú, they *did* look tasty enough to snack on. Unbeknownst to Claire, Blade had helped himself to a cookie as well.

The prep work was going smoothly. This was to be a farewell party for Iona—an event to see her off.

The idea of her blowing herself up all alone in the middle of nowhere was too much for the other students to bear, and they had joined together and convinced her to stay. Guardians had enough energy in their bodies that Iona's detonation could level a small town. But by now, the Second Proving Ground's magic barrier had been strengthened to a ridiculous degree. According to Eliza's calculations, at maximum output, the barrier would be sufficient to contain the explosion. She'd promised to cut her own throat if she was wrong, so everyone felt they could probably trust her math.

They had all racked their brains for a way to save Iona. First, they considered Claire's restoration ability. Unfortunately, Iona's self-destruct sequence was so thorough that it was as good as total annihilation. It had to be, to maintain confidentiality. That meant Claire was useless; her magic couldn't create something out of nothing.

In order to find a solution, Blade had ventured all the way down to the Royal Forbidden Library, the place Iona knew as the "central control room." It was already being protected by a new Guardian—Iona's little sister, perhaps. He felt a tad guilty, but he still blew it to bits. However, all his research led to the same conclusion—that there was no way to save Iona. Any unit that disconnected from Mother was destined to self-destruct.

By the time the students accepted the truth, there were only ten hours left. In the end, they decided to remain with Iona right up to the last possible moment. They'd all stay together until it was time for her to self-destruct—and then they'd watch it happen. At that point, they'd be on the other side of the barrier, still physically close to Iona (no more than a few yards away) as they shared in her last few seconds.

"Don't just stand there, Blade. You need to help, too."

Blade looked up at the sound of Earnest's voice. She had a hand on her curvy hip, a hard look in her eyes. He waved back at her.

"Sorry. I've got a lot to do…"

"What, exactly?"

"I'm gonna go see the king real quick."

"W-wait! Blade?!"

Blade left Earnest standing in the middle of the Proving Ground and didn't return.

○ Scene XIX: The Countdown

Ugggh, what is Blade up to?

The party kept going as Earnest agonized over Blade's whereabouts.

They'd wound up kicking off the festivities without him. There were all kinds of treats—meat, drinks, fruit, sweets, and even a cake. Volunteers performed acrobatic leaps and magic tricks. Someone attempted a comedy act, though it was mostly met with boos. A few among the audience gave the comedian a collective thumbs-down and called for his formal execution. That, at least, got some laughter.

Iona was currently haranguing the would-be comedian (it was Clay), asking him what was meant to be funny about his stand-up routine. This proved even more damaging than the booing.

Sophie was constantly by the android's side, while Earnest was a step behind them, taking in the scene. This was the role Blade normally occupied—his usual vantage point when he was with other people. Someone needed to watch over everyone and ensure this mission was a success. She really wanted to jump in and enjoy herself, but with Blade gone, she was forced to take his place.

Ugh, what the heck is he doing?

The clock was ticking. Iona was keeping the countdown visible on her forehead, and there were only two hundred or so ticks left. Earnest didn't want to think about how many minutes remained.

Just then, she noticed Yessica sneaking back into the party.

"Did you find him?" she asked.

"No. He must have left the academy."

Yessica was aiming to be a spy. If she couldn't find him, he must not be there.

"Where the heck did that idiot wander off to?"

"He must have abandoned the lot of you and run away," said Asmodeus. *"Surprisingly heartless of him, no?"*

"Shut up, you fool! He'd *never* do something like that!"

Earnest started slapping her sword. She couldn't believe he'd say something so ridiculous. Just then, she noticed Yessica looking at her, smiling warmly.

"W-wait! No! I... It's not what it sounds like! It's just... *Ugh*, this stupid *thing*...!"

"Okay. Sure. It's fine. I understand."

Thanks to Asmodeus, Yessica had gotten the wrong idea, and Earnest suspected she'd never manage to set things straight.

"Oh, hey! They're going to cut the cake!"

A huge cake was placed in the center of the party area—the latest masterpiece from Madam in the cafeteria kitchen. It was Iona's job to cut it.

With a few *thwap*s, she whipped the feelers on the back of her neck toward the cake, and in an instant it was cut into 113 equal portions—one for Blade, Cú, herself, Ein, Zwei, and the 108 students of Rosewood Academy. Then her hands ferried each piece off to its recipient.

Everyone stared at the cake Iona had just cut for them.

"Please, go ahead and eat," she said.

But nobody could. Not even Cú the living garbage disposal. Even Earnest, always first in line for any dessert, couldn't stand to take a bite. Everyone knew that by the time they finished eating it, Iona would be about to self-destruct. They all stared reluctantly at their plates. Though of course, refusing to eat wasn't going to stop time.

Earnest stood wavering in front of her plate, just like everyone else.

That idiot. Blade, that absolute moron.

Rage, directed at Blade, bubbled up inside of her. He must have been sulking over Iona going away and refused to stick around for her farewell party.

I didn't realize he was such a small-minded idiot. What a disappointment. What a disappointment. What a disappointment. What a disappointment.

"I am sure you will regret thinking that, Master," said Asmodeus.

"Don't give me that crap!"

Earnest gave Asmodeus a few choice whacks.

Men have no delicacy, no matter what they're shaped like!

"C'mon, guys!" she said, raising her voice. "Iona cut this cake for us! Let's all enjoy it!" She issued this order as Empress of the academy—and as Iona's friend.

"Thanks, Madam! Thanks, Iona!"

Chomp. One hundred and eight people, one dragon, and two birds all dug into the cake at once. But Blade wasn't there. He was the only one missing.

He's so stupid! So stupid!

Earnest imagined beating him up in her mind.

○ Scene XX: Self-Destruction

The time had come.

Once the countdown dipped below twenty, everyone suddenly turned dour. It was time to retreat to the other side of the magical barrier, leaving Iona all alone with the tables and the food.

Currently, the number on her head was eighteen. Multiplied by ten, that was 180 seconds—three minutes to go.

A thin, rainbow-tinted film separated everyone from Iona. She was only five or six feet away. They could see her, but they could no longer interact with her.

"It might be better to move farther away," said Iona. "Everyone could get hurt if the explosion proves stronger than expected."

"We want to be as close to you as we can. We want to keep watching you until the end."

"I want the same thing. But..."

"It's fine. Eliza said she'd cut her throat if she got the calculations wrong."

"I will," Eliza said, her expression dead serious.

Iona broke into a smile. "I think, just now, I have gained an understanding of 'humor.' Even at this very moment, I am still growing."

The countdown continued relentlessly as they spoke. Finally, it was down to one digit.

"Thank you very much for today," Iona said. "My last memory will be a good one. At first, I wondered what point there was to recording such a small amount of data when I am soon to disappear forever... But I finally understand. Even if I am gone in a few seconds' time, I am here at this moment. Now that I have entered Stand Alone Mode, become mortal, and am mere seconds from destruction, I feel I have at last come to understand humanity."

"Iona..."

Earnest swore she wouldn't cry. The Empress never cried... But in truth, she hadn't been the Empress for some time. Right now, she was just a girl.

Iona turned to Sophie. "Sophie... Thanks to you, I feel I have become fully human."

"I wish to say the same to you. I, too, was incomplete before."

"Claire, thank you for taking my hand," said Iona. "I still remember how that felt. Yessica, I wish we'd had more time to gossip. Ovie, I leave to you the job of beating my master to death. Clay, Kassim, I wish you would stop staring at breasts all the time. Leonard, if you keep making weird faces, you'll lose all your fans. Cú, I hope you grow up big and strong, no matter how naughty you are."

By the time Iona finished her parting words, the count was down to three. Thirty more seconds...

Iona put the palm of her hand against the inside of the barrier. The thin film reacted to her, generating a few sparks. It didn't bother her at all.

"Earnest... I'm scared," she said.

"Iona…"

Earnest put her palm against the outside of the barrier, overlapping Iona's. More sparks. The barrier was burning her, but she didn't care. Burning was something she was pretty used to by now.

"Earnest…help me…"

They were no more than half an inch apart, but the distance may as well have been infinite.

"I'm sorry… I'm sorry…"

Earnest couldn't do it. She couldn't save Iona. If only she had more power…about as much power as the Hero who'd saved the world… But she wasn't a Hero—not even close. She was just a student, and she couldn't save the girl in front of them, terrified of her imminent death.

Blade. Where are you, Blade…? You're so stupid. Stupid. Stupid…

Earnest crumpled to her knees and fell against the barrier. Sparks flew. Intense pain washed over her—it felt less like she was burning and more like her body was melting from the heat… But her heart hurt far more than the searing pain from the barrier.

Mirroring Iona, she pressed her face against its surface. The number on Iona's head was now *1*. Just ten more seconds.

"Earnest, don't…forget me. Please don't forget me."

"I won't… I'll never, ever forget you!"

As Earnest shouted, the number changed to zero.

Earnest gasped and held her breath. It felt like even her heart had ceased to beat. She willed herself to stop blinking. She had to witness this moment, the moment Iona disappeared…

The moment she—…

The moment she—…

But that moment…

…didn't seem to be coming.

"Phaaah!!"

Earnest, unable to hold her breath any longer, finally exhaled. Nothing was happening. There was no explosion.

Why? What's going on?

"It's been over a minute," Eliza announced.

"...Why is nothing happening?" Earnest mumbled in a daze. She couldn't process what was going on.

Iona was standing on the other side of the barrier, looking a bit out of place. She put her weight on her right foot, then her left, then looked at the others and smiled awkwardly.

"Ahhh! I made it in time!"

Suddenly, Blade's voice rang out. He staggered through the crowd, tipping over in front of Earnest and falling to the ground.

"Wha... What? Blade... Where were you?"

"Oh, um, I heard there was a party... Is there any food left?"

"You're... You're too late!"

"Out of food already? Eesh. How mean. You didn't save any for me?"

"You're calling *us* mean? *Us*?! *You're* the meanest one of all! You didn't even show up for Iona's farewell party! You are beyond late! And now, when you finally *do* arrive, the first thing you ask about is *food*?!"

Earnest grabbed him by the collar and shook vigorously. Whatever Blade had been doing, it had clearly exhausted him. His clothing was in tatters, and his hair was covered in dust...and now Earnest was shaking him around. His head bounced off the ground a few times. She even headbutted him.

"Man, Earnest, you look awful. Have Claire fix you up."

"*I'm* not the one you should be worried about!!"

Another headbutt. Claire came over to restore Earnest's bleeding face. It wouldn't do for a girl to have scars, after all.

"Um, Empress?" Eliza stepped up. "You're free to rough up Blade all you want, but I think we should probably pursue the super-being's potential connection to Iona's countdown stopping."

"Right! Yes! ...Blade! What were you off doing?! If you weren't sulking, what were you up to?!"

"Sulking? What are you talking about?"

Blade frowned at her, clearly sulking. *See?* Earnest thought. *You are sulking!*

"I just...worked stuff out," he said.

"'Worked stuff out'?"

"Yeah. I worked stuff out with her boss. That…thing she calls Mother."

"Huh?" Earnest froze.

"The whole reason Iona was gonna self-destruct…that 'lonely stand' or whatever it's called…was because she got cut off by Mother and stopped being a 'terminal'… So if Mother's behind all of this, I figured I should go see her and try to win her over. So I did."

"Wh-where did you go, exactly?"

Blade pointed a finger toward the ground. *Down…?*

"I managed to persuade her. I had to use my fists, though."

He smiled and clenched his hands into fists.

I don't think that's called "persuasion"… But then, Blade wasn't sulking at all… He went off by himself to rescue Iona…and he actually did it…

"*I told you, Master, that you would regret looking down on him later,*" said Asmodeus.

"Well, you need to be *clearer* when you say stuff like that!"

She slammed her fist against the sword at her waist. She could sense everyone's lukewarm smiles on her, but she just couldn't stop herself.

"My connection with Mother has been restored," said Iona. "She is still not responding to my queries, but my device authentication has been approved. I do not detect anything that could trigger the self-destruct program at this time."

"Umm…" Earnest was still a little fuzzy on what was going on.

"She means we're out of danger, Earnest," said Sophie. "So let go of Blade's head, would you?"

"Oh. Sorry." Earnest followed her advice, and Blade's head thudded to the ground.

"Oww…"

"Oh. Sorry."

"Is it okay to turn the barrier off now?" Eliza asked.

Iona was hopping around excitedly on the other side, as if she was warming up for something.

"All right. Do it," said Earnest.

The barrier disappeared. And the moment it did—

"Masterrrrrrrrrrr!"

—Iona grabbed Blade and hugged him with tremendous force.

"Hey! Stop it! Get off me! My whole body hurts! My ribs, my ribs! They're broken!"

Earnest looked on and smiled. Normally, she'd be scolding Iona and telling her to back off. But for today, she decided to be lenient.

"Master! Master, Master! Masterrrr!!"

Or so she'd thought...

"Master! Master! Masterrrrrr!"

She was running out of patience fast.

"...Hey, Iona? Hey. That's enough, don't you think? How about you step away for a bit?"

"Master! Masterrrr! Masterrrrrrrrrr!"

Iona had her entire body smushed against Blade's, her large breasts pushing down hard enough to crush him.

"Hey! Get off! Get off him! Get off right *nowwwwww*!"

Earnest's screams echoed across the Proving Ground.

Chapter 3:
Looking for Something Tastier than Me

○ Scene I: The Royal Larder

"Five of you! Go in from the right! Three of you, come with me!"

Blade and his party were hunting a gigantic beast. They had driven it out from the thick jungle and into a more open rocky area, where they would finish it off.

The beast itself was a strange specimen. It was a predator, about ten yards long...or tall, depending on how you looked at it, and it had four legs, only two of which it used to stand. Even Blade, who had traveled all across the land, had never seen anything like it. Its jaws alone made up a good third of its size—big enough to swallow a grown man in one gulp. Its long tail was thicker than it was tall. These two features served as its natural weapons. It was also quick, though that was nothing they couldn't handle.

"Okay, okay, over here!"

Yessica manipulated her seven-colored elemental power in a bid to attract the giant creature's attention. It readily accepted her challenge. She would be the decoy, leading the beast into the pitfall trap they'd set up in advance. Once it fell in, the rest would be easy—and that day's dinner would be served.

"Gwaaaaaaargh!"

The beast howled. This was no magical creature, though. A magical creature this strong would possess intelligence and be capable of understanding speech. This guy was definitely working on animal instinct alone. It was just a strong—and very tasty—wild beast.

Then, all of a sudden, the situation changed.

"Huh? Hey! Over here, over here! *Here!*"

The beast ignored Yessica and suddenly altered its course. It seemed to have found something even more appetizing. It was headed straight for—

"Claire! Run!"

Blade jumped out and pushed Claire away from the beast's jaws, just barely missing them himself. But he couldn't avoid the tail whip that came straight afterward. The blow hit him hard. It felt like colliding head-on with a carriage.

Blade was sent flying through the air, wondering:

How the heck did I end up here?

o Scene II: One Week Ago, at the Dining Hall

Blade was having his usual lunch in the dining hall, as always.

He was sitting alone at the large table, eating his favorite katsu curry. Normally, he'd be surrounded by other students, but today he was the only one there. Why? Because everyone was over at Dione's table instead.

Instructors ate in the same dining hall as the students, but since Dione also served as an active general, she was very busy and didn't often appear at the academy. From what Blade had heard, she made trips out to the kingdom's frontier and back twice a week. It had to be hundreds of miles from her post to the capital, but apparently she was able to run the distance in a single night. Maybe that was to be expected from a centaur champion.

Today, however, Dione was enjoying a nice, leisurely lunch. The girls crowded around her, carrots in hand, hoping for a chance to feed her. The guys joined them, hoping instead to have a look at her breasts. Earnest and her gang were there for yet another reason—to hear more stories from Blade's younger years.

And so Blade was eating his katsu curry all by himself. Sophie, Iona, and even Cú were absent. He was completely, utterly alone.

"So you don't know when Blade's birthday is?" someone asked.

"That's right," Dione answered. "I don't even know his exact age. When they found him, he was already walking on his own. If he was around one year old then, that would make him seventeen."

What, are other people deciding my age, now?

"Wow, so even Blade doesn't know what day he was born?"

No, I don't. Sorry.

"I guess we can't celebrate it, then..."

It's not like I've ever celebrated it before. I've had to fight every single day since I was (approximately) one year old.

Blade was silently chewing his curry, listening to bits and pieces of the conversation. Then Sophie came back and sat down—right next to him, for some reason.

"Oh?" he asked. "Are you sure you don't wanna hang out with Dione?"

"I saw you sulking over here."

"Ah..."

Was I that obvious? I'll have to be more careful.

"You know," continued Dione, "when they found Blade at one year old, he was carrying a sword with him."

"Oh, I knew that. Blade told me himself."

"Wow. So if he was carrying a spear, would he be called 'Lance' instead? Or if he'd had a cudgel, would he be named 'Cudgel'?"

"Ah-ha-ha-ha-ha-ha! That's *so* funny!"

Yessica was doubled over laughing.

Hi! I am Cudgel! Nice to meet you!

"Hey, Blade." Suddenly, Earnest was talking to him. "Stop making faces and sulking like that."

Who's sulking? Not me.

"Blade, what would you like for a birthday present?"

"Katsu curry," he replied glumly.

"What? What are you, stupid?"

"What's the problem? It's good. I like it."

"Ha-ha-ha!" The king roared with laughter as he entered the dining hall. "I heard that! And no need to ask—I'll tell you! I've been listening in ever since Sophie said, 'I saw you sulking over here'!" *What nonsense. No one asked him anything.* "Ah, youth! Absolutely wonderful!"

"Go away, old man," Blade said coldly.

By now everybody in the academy knew what kind of things happened when this man was in a jolly mood. They had all found out the hard way. Some of the more quick-witted students were already putting away their dishes and preparing to make a mad dash for the exit.

"Oh, don't be so grumpy," said the king. "You were just talking about your favorite food, weren't you? Yes, yes, everyone has a few top picks. So do I, in fact. Wonderful! In that case, I hereby grant you permission for some very realistic practical training down in the Royal Larder!"

Those words were what started it all.

Blade watched as the doors closed.

They were gigantic—over a hundred feet tall—and made of unknown metal. Layer upon layer came out from all four directions, ostentatiously locking the students inside.

With a heavy thud, the last of the layers finished securing the exit, and Blade turned back toward his party.

"Well, ready to go?"

No amount of staring at the doors was going to make them open back up. In times like this, you had to face forward and work through your problems. That's what he'd always done back when he was a Hero.

"You don't seem too bothered by any of this," said Earnest.

"Hmm?"

"Never mind."

Earnest started to say something, then gave up. *If she has something to say, she should just say it,* he thought.

"In order to reopen these doors, you'll have to meet the conditions,"

said the king. "Until you all consume a combined total of 11.3 billion calories, they won't budge an inch."

For this expedition, at least, the king was joining them—him and his
twelve female attendants, along with Dione. That, and one more person—
the dining hall's head cook, a middle-aged lady that everyone called Madam.

As for the students… Blade had thought that was a weird number of
calories to specify. But it was just simple math. In the end, the total worked
out to 100 million calories per person. Every student at the academy was
in on this training, and that meant *everyone* on the Rosewood student rolls.
Blade and the other 108 students were all there, plus the "special" students—
one dragon, one android, and two birds.

All of them were staring at the doors, looking disheartened after being
told they might never open again.

It was possible that, if they grabbed the king, held him down, and
pressed his royal crest against the latch, they could get out immediately…
Or they could simply complete the mission.

"This is not a drill! I repeat, this is not a drill!"

What was the king on about now? Hadn't he just said this would be
more practical training? Wasn't a drill just training? *So is this training or
not? Be clear! Not that I care…*

Before them was a dense jungle. They were underground, but the foli-
age was as thick as anything on the outside—and there was even a blue sky
above them. Ein and Zwei were flying around in it, squawking excitedly.

This was the so-called Royal Larder, the site of the student body's latest
"practical training" session.

○ Scene III: The Camp

"Heyyy! We're back!"

Carrying their catch, Blade's party made their way back to the camp
where the others were waiting. Ahead, they could see the high fences
surrounding their base; a sentry waved at them, and the large gate started
to open.

Blade's team had brought back the ingredients for that night's dinner.

It would have been impossible to transport the gigantic beast in one piece, so they had chopped it up into several large chunks and carried it that way.

"Ugh," shouted Yessica, "I am *drenched* in blood! I need a bath *so* bad!"

"I think the hot-spring corps probably have the thermae going by now," Blade replied.

As he spoke, a column of hot water gushed into the air, spraying high above the camp's fence.

"See?" he said, turning around and winking at his team.

"My, my! How shall I prepare all this?"

Madam was clearly excited to receive their delivery. She was already swinging a butcher knife as big as a longsword. Then again, it wasn't like she could use a normal kitchen knife to chop up hunks of meat this humongous.

After handing over their catch to Madam, Blade wandered around the camp. Only two parties, twelve people in total, had gone out to hunt that day. The others were working hard setting up camp—chopping down trees from the jungle and using them to build temporary shelters, then surrounding it all with a fence and digging a thermae…

Maybe this really *was* practical training. Fighting was far from a soldier's only job on the front lines. They had to build camps, too—something their classes had never previously touched on.

"Hey, Blade."

Earnest called out to Blade as he passed by. She was carrying blueprints.

She'd taken command of the camp. After all, she had a knack for internal administration, and once the Empress had a few choice words with someone, they never wanted to slack off again. Under her rule, the camp's total labor output had improved by 200 percent.

"I heard you've been busy," she said.

"Yeah. I went flying, in fact."

"...You went flying?"

Earnest looked doubtful. To demonstrate, Blade spread his arms out and flapped them a few times.

"Well... Good work. The bath's ready, so go ahead and get in."

He'd seen the plume of hot water earlier, and apparently the bath was already open for business. The students had managed to locate the hot spring quickly and precisely thanks to Iona's "day-tuh-base" or whatever it was, so the digging hadn't taken much time.

"Good heavens, Earnest. That's simply not fair!" said the king. "When I asked you, you said the bath wasn't ready yet. You did! I swear you did! I heard it myself!"

He was sitting with a beautiful woman on either side of him, kicking his legs and throwing a tantrum.

"Your Majesty, you are merely an observer here. I have taken command, and you must therefore follow my instructions... Also, to be frank, if you're just going to eat, sleep, and flirt all day instead of working, I'd appreciate it if you would at least keep quiet. Do you understand?"

"Heyyy! Earnest is bullying me! Sirene!"

"There, there, sire..."

The king buried his face in Sirene's chest and let out a few fake sobs. The sight of a grown man behaving this way had Earnest gritting her teeth in rage.

Then, all of a sudden, her expression changed, and she smiled warmly at Blade.

"So, yes, Blade. You can enter the bath first."

"Um, okay..."

Unable to say no to Earnest's smile, Blade hurried to the hot spring.

o Scene IV: The Thermae

"Whew…"

Blade leaned back in the open-air bath, a dry hand towel folded neatly atop his head.

The public bath up on the surface was so huge that you couldn't see from one end to the other. But down here, you could turn your head a bit and take in the whole thing easily. It couldn't fit everybody at once, but as long as people took turns, it never got too crowded.

This was the only bath in the camp, and it was mixed gender, of course. With their limited resources, a single bath was the best they could do.

If the students hadn't gotten used to mixed-gender bathing on the surface, Blade suspected they would have had a lot of screaming and shouting, but by now nobody was bothered. Some of the boys would still hunch over and make themselves look as inconspicuous as possible, but that was about it.

When Blade thought about it, having a hot spring in such an inhospitable area was downright luxurious.

This place was known as the Royal Larder. It was located directly under the royal palace, not very deep underground. It was above both the Royal Forbidden Library and the place that held Mother, to whom Blade had so rudely introduced himself not long ago.

Blade had been through this area many times, but he had never realized just how enormous it was. In fact, it was far larger than made logical sense. After all, it had a "sky" broad enough for clouds to form. Mountains, no doubt thousands of feet high, were visible in the distance…but they had only gone down six hundred feet or so. Why weren't those clouds and mountain peaks poking through the ground?

It seemed reasonable to conclude that the doors they'd passed through connected to another dimension. Magic which "folded" up space into a more compact area had supposedly been quite common back in the Age of Divinity.

It was no mistake that this place was called the Royal Larder. As it happened, this was where the people from that ancient age stored their food. It looked a little different now, though. Blade didn't know just how much time had passed since the Age of Divinity, but after so many years, it seemed the plants and animals had all escaped and formed their own ecosystem.

Large-scale hunts had to be conducted regularly to keep everything under control, but the food thriving here was all incredibly strong—a party of six champions was the standard team for a hunting run. That said, while one or two champions might be able to step away from the front lines at a time, not even the king could force six to abandon their posts at once. As a result, there hadn't been any hunts—or "spring cleanings," as some called them—for quite some time. That was how the task had fallen to Blade and the other Rosewood Academy students.

"I can't believe he's making the students fill the shoes of six whole champions," Blade grumbled.

"Yeah, I know."

"...Whuh?"

Blade had thought he was alone. When he heard the response, he whipped around to find Earnest's red-tinted silhouette.

She had a towel pressed against her body, and her face was slightly flushed. Why was she so red? She hadn't started soaking in the water yet... Could she be embarrassed?

She had mostly overcome her hang-ups about mixed bathing, but maybe she still felt a tad awkward about it. She had no problem standing strong and tall in front of people like Leonard, but whenever Blade was around, she'd blush and try to hide her body. It made no sense to him.

"Hey, you're not supposed to dip your towel in the water," he said.

"I—I know that...!"

Earnest twisted her hair up and secured it at the back of her head. It looked the same as when Blade first met her—back when she was the Empress.

Girls sometimes put their hair up like that, don't they? Like when they go in the bath and tie it up in a bun... Oh, that must be what they do when they're not washing it. It's gotta be a real hassle to wash when it gets that long. Wow, I'm so smart!

"Just…don't look at me too much, all right?"

With that, Earnest peeled the towel off her body.

"I won't," Blade promised.

He wasn't like Clay or Kassim or Leonard. He didn't even try to glance at her out of the corner of his eye. He hadn't lied.

Blade never stared at other guys who were naked in the bath. Why would he stare at girls? He didn't really understand what made women's bodies different from men's.

"Wow… You really *aren't* looking, are you?"

"Do you want me to look or not?" Blade shot back, unable to stop himself.

"Well, whatever," said Earnest. "Go lie down over there."

"Huh? What for?"

Earnest had pointed to a large, flat rock in the middle of the bath, about the size and shape of a bed. Blade followed her instructions, not understanding what she wanted. The stone was warm to the touch from all the hot water around it.

"I want to give you a massage…to thank you for your help with today's hunt."

Huh? What? What's happening? Earnest is doing something nice for me? She's giving me a massage?

Blade lay flat on his stomach, confused, as Earnest straddled his back. Then she began to rub.

Whoa. She really is giving me a massage. And she's good at it, too. Her hands pressed down, not too soft and not too hard, giving Blade's muscles exactly the relaxing sort of touch they needed.

As she moved from his back to his shoulders, Blade felt something soft and elastic press against his spine.

"They're hitting me," he said, letting her know. He didn't mind at all… but he knew by now that Earnest probably would.

"I'm doing that on purpose," she said.

Oh? Why?

"You've been sulking a lot lately, haven't you, Blade?"

Earnest stopped the massage and traced a number of the old scars on his back. Her cheek, and her breasts, pressed against his skin as her fingertips crawled up and down his back. She was practically entwining her body with his, like they were lovers. Not that he knew anything about how lovers acted. At any rate, he was more interested in what Earnest was saying.

"What do you mean? I was sulking? *Me?*"

"Yeah. Because we talked about your birthday and stuff."

"Mmm? Oh… That time at the dining hall."

The others had asked when his birthday was, and he said he didn't know. And it was true. He didn't.

"And," she continued, prodding his scars, "His Majesty was super annoying just now, wasn't he?"

"He's always annoying… And isn't that rude of you to say?"

Earnest was always quick to accuse Blade of being "disrespectful" whenever he badmouthed the king…but hadn't she been treating him a lot worse earlier? Thanks to her, though, Blade's irritation with the old man had subsided somewhat.

But… Oh. Is that why?

"So…what does that have to do with you putting your breasts on my body?"

"Nothing," Earnest said. Her face still wasn't visible, but the supple bulges pressed against his back felt a little warmer now. "All right. That's all the special service you're getting."

She moved away. So that was some kind of service? She'd even called it special. But how was it serving him, exactly?

Blade rotated his shoulders. The massage had certainly done the trick. Earnest's spirit was infused with a small amount of flame, so whenever she touched him, it accelerated his blood circulation and made his skin feel pleasantly toasty.

"Thanks, Earnest. I feel better."

"Are you done sulking, then?"

"Yeah."

He didn't recall doing any sulking, but he nodded anyway. He appreciated the massage, and while he didn't know if it was thanks to Earnest or not, Blade finally felt a little enthusiastic about tackling this round of practical training.

○ Scene V: The Daily Hunts

They went hunting again the next day, under a blue sky that seemed to go on endlessly.

Blade and his team were on top of a rocky hill, surveying the area. By now the students were pretty used to hunting. They'd been honing their group combat skills for a while now. They worked in teams of six called "platoons." Several of those formed a company, and several companies formed a battalion. Their training had taught them how to fight in groups like this organically.

First, they'd worked together to defeat Cú, the baby dragon. After that, they'd fended off the spirit birds attacking the capital. And now they were putting all that experience to the test in this new, unfamiliar land.

Thanks to their teamwork, they'd already eliminated almost every major threat. There was just one problem: There was no longer enough prey to go around.

Up above, Ein and Zwei were circling and squawking—hungry and worked up, no doubt. Blade's team felt exactly the same. But there was no prey in sight. It looked like they had hunted everything they could in this area—or else all the animals had already fled in fear.

Unlike the magic beasts up on the surface, the creatures of this world— the alternate dimension called the Larder—seemed to have an emotion commonly known as fear. They were all insanely strong, but when faced with anything more powerful, they got frightened and ran away.

"Maybe it was a bad idea to just eat everything in sight," Blade said to Earnest next to him. "We probably should've planned this out better and taken a more sustainable approach."

"Rrrrrrh... Hun...gry..."

"Human language, please," he said, tapping her on the head with his scabbard. "And stop walking on all fours. Stand up."

"Huh? What?"

That snapped Earnest out of her trance, and she got to her feet. Whenever she ran low on calories, she would lose all sense of reason and start acting like a wild animal.

"I can't believe you go feral after missing a single meal. Shouldn't you work on that? You know, with some spiritual training or something?"

"Sh-shut up, all right? That was just...a fluke..."

"Earnest, you're drooling," said Sophie.

Earnest hurriedly wiped her mouth with the back of her hand. Then she fixed her posture, thighs taut and back straight. Instead of her usual red outfit, she was wearing a more primitive garment made of animal skin wrapped around her waist and chest. The other girls were dressed the same way, while the guys made do with just loincloths.

It was pretty much the Stone Age around here, and not just in terms of their clothing. They were using handmade weapons as well, crafted from the horns, bones, and teeth of the giant beasts they'd defeated. One person carried a sword made of bone, another a spear made from a giant antler, a club fashioned from a femur, and so on.

These weapons were actually pretty decent. Some of the students performed better with them than with their original weapons. Once his current sword wore out, Blade was thinking about having the next one made from bone. After several days of hunting and intense combat, everyone's usual array of weapons and armor had long since fallen apart. The only exceptions were Earnest and Leonard's magical gear, which was a lot tougher than anything else. No matter how much it was used and abused, it stayed in top condition.

"You know," said Earnest, Asmodeus strapped to her shoulder, "you're the only one here who still looks mostly civilized."

"Huh? Me?" said Blade.

He examined himself. He was still sporting his school uniform, along with a plain, ultra-blunt sword provided by the academy. His clothes were a bit scruffy, but still presentable. He hadn't been attacked all that much since coming here, and when he was, he made an effort to parry the blows away from him. He also took pains to treat his sword gently to prevent breakage—part of his new normal-person routine.

"You're the only one, Blade. It's not fair."

"It's not?"

In Blade's opinion, Earnest's current outfit wasn't half-bad. He thought the wild look suited her.

"Master," Iona said, "I have detected a swarm via ground radar."

She had her right knee on the ground and her left knee up, an ear-shaped antenna whirling around above her head. The antenna had now stopped and was pointing in a single direction.

"Honored Father! There's a big herd over there!"

Cú's voice came down from above. Ein and Zwei were squawking as well. Cú was still mostly in human form with only her wings out. She was getting better and better at assuming her half-dragon form, which allowed her to manifest parts of her dragon form without fully switching over.

She and Iona had reached the same conclusion, so it was time to move.

"Great! Roger that! Good job!"

Blade waved his arm in a circular motion to signal Cú.

"I have not received any praise, Master," Iona politely pointed out. *What a pain.*

"Right! Let's head for the herd!"

"Let's gooo!!"

With that shout from the cavegirl Empress, they all scrambled down the cliff.

○ Scene VI: The Way Back

Blade's team was now on their way back, their catch hoisted above their heads. The campsite was off in the distance; the smoke from its cooking fires was visible for miles around, making it easy to find.

"Ugh, I am *drenched* in blood… I need a bath…"

"Same here…"

"And here…"

"Over here, too…"

Earnest lodged the first complaint and Yessica agreed, then Sophie and Ovie joined in.

Each of them was holding a hunk of meat weighing several hundred pounds. They were using a special technique that gave them super strength, originally developed by Claire, who had then taught it to everyone else. The key was learning how to control your spirit correctly, but as of yet, no one could match Claire in terms of power and duration. Only the android Iona, who could carry over a ton with her base specs alone, could manage a bigger load.

Blade stared at Iona, marveling at how she could carry a hunk of meat the size of a large bolder above her head. *How does she keep it balanced?*

"I am a high-spec machine," she explained.

"I didn't say anything. And I wasn't praising you."

"Should I have said that I desired a bath, too, Master? Would you like to join me?"

"I won't stop you from going in, but I'm not required to join you."

Ever since Blade had "talked things over" with Mother and saved Iona from self-destruction, she had grown oddly fond of him. She was always waiting for Blade to praise her, but he was too embarrassed to, so he kept curtly brushing her off instead. Whenever this happened, everyone around them would start to giggle. *I wonder why?*

"No eating that, Cú," admonished Claire. "That's raw."

"Aww, but raw's the best!" she replied. "Don't you people know that?"

The chunk of flesh in Cú's arms was now around half of its original size. She'd been eating it along the way.

"Our catch today was equivalent to an estimated fifty million calories," said Iona. "That number has now shrunk to approximately 49,800,000 calories."

"Cú, stop. It'll be more fun if you eat dinner with the rest of the gang."

"I… I'll try!"

They were almost back at camp.

○ Scene VII: The King's Order

"Open the gate, please!"

"Open the gate!"

The guard atop the gate saw Earnest and gave the command. The signal made its way to several others—"Open the gate," "They said to open it," "Open it up!"—and then the gears turned, the ropes tightened, and the gate slowly lifted.

As soon as Blade's team came in, everyone raised a cheer for them and the meat they'd brought. They felt like champions after a triumphant return, and they spent a few moments soaking in the atmosphere.

But then, their faces turned bitter in an instant. The king had come to personally greet them, and he was rubbing his hands together like he had a favor to ask.

"What is it, Your Majesty?" Earnest said, her voice hard. She'd just left her portion of meat with a girl from the cooking team.

"I see the hunting is going well."

"As of today, we have reached forty-seven percent of our goal," said Iona. "Assuming we maintain our current pace, it will take approximately twelve days to reach the requested 11.3 billion calories."

Iona was good at doing all these minute calculations, and she'd take advantage of this "high-spec" ability to constantly show off, whether anyone had asked her to or not.

"Mmm, yes, remarkable progress. Very, *very* good!"

The king was in high spirits—which meant they were all in imminent danger, as Blade and everyone else now thoroughly understood. Whenever the king was in a good mood, bad things were sure to follow.

"The efficiency of our hunting has improved by an estimated thirteen percent," Iona continued. "But I suppose that's to be expected with a high-spec machine like myself present."

Iona hadn't been at the academy long, so perhaps certain truths hadn't dawned on her yet. She was bragging about her abilities, looking for praise from the king. *Does it not matter who praises her? She's even fine with the old man?*

"Why, at this rate," said the king, "we'd wind up going home earlier than originally planned, wouldn't we?"

Oh, great. Here he goes. Rather than "we'll wind up going home," he'd said "we'd wind up going home." *Would* instead of *will.* It was a subtle difference, but Blade, along with the other 108 students and one dragon, couldn't overlook it. Immediately, everyone's faces fell.

"And so," the king said, face glowing as if he had just come up with a brilliant plan, "I have written up this list."

He then brought out a sheaf of papers.

"Ladies and gentlemen, I would like you to gather the ingredients in this catalog for me."

Great. He just raised the bar again. We finally got our footing and were sprinting toward the finish, and now he ups the challenge level…

…Okay, so maybe that is *how training is supposed to work.*

The students might be stuck in the lost dimension of the Royal Larder, forced to fend for themselves, their weapons and armor depleted and replaced with stone axes and femur clubs, enjoying the simple life of the caveman, but this was still a class—it was still a practical training exercise.

So…maybe this is exactly how it was supposed to go.

Blade turned around and looked at the other students' faces.

Yep. Just as he'd thought. Their expressions all said, "I'm gonna *kill* this old man someday."

Back in his Hero days, Blade used to make faces like that at the king all the time.

○ **Scene VIII: The Emperor Cabbage**

The first item in the catalog was cabbage. Hunting one down would be their first mission.

"Wow…"

The king had handed a datasheet out to everyone with a description of each of their targets and their corresponding habitats. Blade and most of the rest of the student body headed out, leaving only those not suited to combat at camp. Soon, they arrived at the specified location.

"That's…a cabbage, all right."

"Yep. A cabbage."

"Totally a cabbage."

"My analysis indicates that this is a cabbage."

"I prefer meat!"

Everyone offered their opinion—Blade, Earnest, Sophie, Iona, then Cú.

They were all deep inside a cave, far removed from the sun. And yet, for some reason, a gigantic head of cabbage was sitting there all by itself.

"Cabbage" was really the only way to describe it. It was covered in tightly packed, lush green leaves. They looked incredibly delicious—the students couldn't help imagining how sweet they would be, despite this being a vegetable.

This was no ordinary cabbage, of course. First off, it was too big—at least six feet in diameter. Second, it had tendrils growing around it, and they were striking the ground like cracking whips.

The cabbage glared at the students and opened what must have been its mouth.

"*Screeeeeee!*"

"It just screeched at us," said Blade.

"It sure did," Earnest agreed, equally stunned.

"It's trying to intimidate us," observed Sophie.

"Based on the screech's volume and pitch, and our current situation," said Iona, "there is a ninety-eight percent probability that was meant as a threat."

Unfazed, Cú threatened the cabbage right back. "You're just a vegetable! How dare you threaten me! Raaaaaaagh! How do you like that?"

Blade checked the catalog again.

"Um… Let's see. The Emperor Cabbage is an ancestor of the modern cabbage that was stored inside the Royal Larder and has since gone wild and evolved to cope in its harsh new environment."

"Looks…strong, doesn't it?" ventured Earnest.

Blade then read out the "strength" section of the king's datasheet. "Strength, approximately 2.5 dragons."

"*Dragons?* Is that a unit of measurement?"

"I dunno… Probably means it's as strong as that many dragons, right?"

If so, the students had gotten at least that strong some time ago. All 108 of them had banded together to defeat Cú, and everyone was a fair amount stronger by now, so 2.5 dragons didn't seem like that much of a threat…

"I wonder if that thing tastes any good," Earnest mused.

"Tastiness…is also listed on here. It says 2.5 dragons."

"Just what the heck is a *dragon*, then? It's a measure of tastiness, too?"

"I'm just reading what it says."

"I see… It must be some kind of ultimate food."

"It can be inferred that there exists a roughly proportional relationship in this world between the fighting power of a living organism and the density of its flavor," explained Iona. "The standard deviation of this normal distribution is 0.5, which indicates a significant correlation."

"You heard her," said Blade.

"So the stronger a creature is, the more delicious it tastes…," Earnest summarized.

Oh, okay. So that's what she meant. Iona's explanations are just too hard without a translator.

"Then would something that rates one dragon be as tasty as, say, the dragon jerky from Cú's tail?" Earnest mused, casting a sidelong glance at Cú.

The baby dragon shivered and scurried behind Blade.

"I dunno," he said. "You're the only one who ate any of that."

"It was an emergency, all right? I'd never even *dream* of eating Cú normally… I swear!"

She glanced at Cú again.

Shiver.

"Stop it," Blade said. "Anyway, let's take this guy out."

Their opponent seemed to be rooted to the ground. If you kept your distance, it couldn't hit you. They were in a roughly circular chamber, with the Emperor Cabbage in the middle. Most of the ground was covered in sand, but there was an area right around their enemy that was completely smooth. That was probably as far as its tendrils could reach.

"B-Blade…y-you go first, okay?" said Earnest. "You're a super-being."

"I keep telling you to stop calling me that."

That said, this *was* the first time anyone was fighting this guy. Blade felt like he should be the one to take the lead. He took a step forward, then another, making his way into the cabbage's zone of defense.

"Oorf!"

Then he was blown away, his body bent in half at the waist. He'd taken a hard hit, probably to the stomach. Even his Hero Eyes couldn't fully track the enemy's strike, which meant it had likely moved faster than the speed of sound.

"Ah-ha-ha-ha-ha! 'Oorf'! He said 'Oorf'!" Earnest was laughing it up.

"Okay, now it's your turn," said Blade.

"Me? All right…"

Asmodeus in hand, Earnest gradually made her way into the enemy's range—

"Yowgh!"

—and was promptly sent flying into the wall of the cave.

"Hey… You all right?" Blade asked instinctively.

He'd been ready to laugh at her, along the lines of "Ah-ha-ha-ha-ha! 'Yowgh'! She said 'Yowgh'!", but when he saw how painfully she'd bounced off the wall, he thought better of it.

"All right… I've had *enough* of this!" Earnest jumped right back to her feet, shouting at the rest of the students. "Leonard, Sophie, Iona, Cú— and anyone else who thinks they can hold up, surround the perimeter! It'll only hit you once! Hold out like your lives depend on it! The rest of you— if the others manage to keep up the perimeter, charge in immediately! Don't worry! There will be an opening of at least half a second!"

Her observations and instructions were right on the mark.

Blade was still lying where he'd fallen after saying "Oorf" earlier. Since Earnest was giving good advice, and everyone else was following it to the letter, he took the opportunity to rest for a while.

"Maria and the magic team, give us some offense! Burn it with flame magic!"

"Whoa, we weren't asked for roast cabbage," said Blade. This last instruction wasn't so spot-on, so he felt he had to speak up.

"Oh, right. Raw! It's no good if we don't capture it raw! Everyone, be careful!"

So began the battle against the Emperor Cabbage. In the end, it lasted about fifteen minutes.

○ Scene IX: The Boxing Corn

On another day, Blade and the others were in the middle of a vast prairie.

They had run through an entire gauntlet of killer plants, such as green peas with auto-aiming crosshairs and tomatoes that ripened by latching on to a person's skin and sucking up their blood. Now they were looking at an endless field of corn. Really, *really* huge corn. The shape of it was familiar enough, but each ear was about the size of a person.

Come to think of it, everything in this world is gigantic. Were all the plants and animals just really big back in the Age of Divinity? Or did they evolve this way for some reason?

There was a veritable forest of corn stalks, all at least as heavy as a person. And right in the middle of it all was a particularly magnificent stalk that seemed to radiate a golden aura.

"Um, apparently this is called a Boxing Corn," Earnest said, reading off the king's catalog. "This is supposed to be corn? What are we meant to use it for? The datasheet says we'll be sprinkling a little bit on top of some salad. Can't we skip this one? ...No?"

"It doesn't matter what you think. It's on the king's list, isn't it? That means we've gotta do it, right?"

Blade would have loved to skip it if they could, but that was out of the question. He looked to Iona, hoping for some backup.

"That is forbidden information. I cannot answer your question."

"Huh?"

"You *idiot!*" Earnest rushed over and covered Iona's mouth with her hands.

"Mmm? Mmm? Mmmmmmm?"

"It's nothing. Don't worry about it, okay, Blade?"

It seemed like they were hiding something. Not that Blade cared.

"By the way, I get that it's corn and everything, but what's with the 'boxing' part?"

"That's a type of melee sport where people throw punches at each other with their bare fists. The catalog says it was practiced in ancient times."

Just then, the golden corncob came off its stalk and stood up. Two arms and two legs sprouted from its body. The corn proceeded to square up, both its hands held in front of its chin, ready to fistfight.

Wait. Does this thing have a chin? It doesn't even have a face.

"You wanna go? Huh? You wanna go?!" Sucked in by the atmosphere, Blade assumed a battle stance of his own.

"Um…it says here that the Boxing Corn is a 'specially harvested ingredient.'"

"Specially harvested?"

"You have to follow a certain procedure to harvest it."

"And what if we don't?"

"Then it won't taste good. It won't become the *ultimate* corn. Do it right, though, and it says you'll enjoy the tastiest, sweetest corn you've ever had in your life."

"Uh-huh."

Blade didn't really like the sound of that. He could already imagine the king, being spoon fed by one of his female associates and saying *Mmm, yummy in my tummy*. It made Blade want to go on a murderous rampage.

The Boxing Corn began to show off some light, rhythmic footwork, its body bobbing up and down as it danced around Blade.

"Whoa, what's it doing? It's like it's locked on to me…"

"Oh no. Blade, it says here that the first person who makes contact with it has to take it down."

"You should've said so earlier!" Blade unsheathed his sword.

"Wait. No swords. You have to do it with your bare hands."

"What? Then let's get Sophie or Iona in here."

"We can't. There are no substitutions allowed. You already started it."

"Aww, come on…!"

Blade reluctantly threw his sword to the side. The rest of the group scrambled to take it for him, but Iona used her high-spec capabilities to snatch it first.

"One round is three minutes, and then you'll have a one-minute interval. This goes on for up to fifteen rounds. You've got to keep the fight going until the end to make the corn go up in a white-hot blaze... Until the end?"

"Wait, you mean I'm not allowed to win?!" Blade felt himself being plunged into the depths of despair. "And fifteen three-minute rounds? How many minutes *is* that?!"

"That is rudimentary multiplication, Master. It is forty-five minutes. Sixty minutes counting the intervals."

"Oh, okay! Thanks, high-spec machine!"

The first round began.

Some time later, the fifteenth round...came to an end.

Blade slumped to the ground. The Boxing Corn had been incredibly powerful, despite being an ear of corn—a mere vegetable. Blade figured it had to rate around three dragons, at least. Using a different scale, it would rate one champion, since a champion was supposed to be as strong as three dragons. If you were surrounded by three dragons and couldn't get out alive, you couldn't call yourself a champion.

Taking on an enemy with the fighting strength of three dragons—barehanded, mind you—was just a little too much for a retired, broken-down ex-Hero. Blade couldn't even bust out 15 percent of his full power. He might not even rate one whole champion.

But then again, his opponent had struggled just as much with him.

"Looks like the super-being was a bit too much for the king of the cornfield to handle," Eliza said as she adjusted her glasses.

The catalog was not using metaphor—his opponent really *had* burned up in a white-hot blaze. Its husk had turned to ash, revealing the dazzling gold cob inside. Then it started to shed its kernels.

"Okay, grab them!"

At Earnest's signal, the girls mobbed the Boxing Corn's remains, grabbing as many kernels as they could.

"Good job, Blade."

She patted him on the shoulder and smiled. The sensation reminded Blade of something.

"Hey, could you give me that special massage service again?"

"Whuh— Blade! D-don't talk about that! *Shhhhh!!*"

"Oh, was that a secret?"

"Ooh, what's up? Is this a special service we're talking about? ♡" Yessica loomed over Earnest.

"Y-Yessica, d-don't make it sound like something filthy…!"

Maria immediately undid her braids, transforming into Ovie. "I think it's time to get to the bottom of just how filthy this 'special service' is."

"If it makes Blade feel good, I am fine with it," said Sophie, chiming in.

"Yeah, it made me feel great!"

"Whoa! Blade!" Earnest was panicking.

Blade, however, wasn't sure what everyone was so worked up about. *Can't we just pick up this corn and go?*

○ Scene X: Gathering Ingredients

The students kept on hunting down ingredients.

Flour, yeast, rice, potatoes—they all had their own quirks to handle. All of them attacked, despite mostly being plants; even the yeast, clearly defined as bacteria, showed signs of intelligence.

It had covered the ground like a vast, slippery slime, which had made for a rough bout. They'd had to fight billions of tiny, near-invisible beings at once…and even worse, each one was intelligent enough to take possession of its adversaries' minds, controlling them like puppets.

Try to burn them down, with either a magic fireball or Earnest's fire breath, and they'd just multiply and replenish their numbers. Earnest, incidentally, could breathe fire when she was in Scion mode. In the ex-Hero's eyes, she was basically classified as a monster now.

So how did they beat the yeast? Well, Iona was the one who did it, using something she called "offensive nanomachines" to infiltrate and erode the bacteria. The way it worked was…a little beyond Blade. In the end, she just flashed them all a smug smile and said, "Well, I *am* a high-spec machine," and everyone showered her with praise.

After that, they placed a small sample of the killer yeast into a test tube for safekeeping, though Blade had no idea what they were going to use it for.

There were tons of other killer plants, too. For example, the sunflower that concentrated the power of sunlight inside itself and shot it back out as a laser beam. That beam had been *hot*. Obtaining the sunflower seeds on the king's list had been a struggle of epic proportions.

Elsewhere, they faced off against a chili pepper with an evil-looking face. It was a giant, red, ripe pepper that kept grinning maniacally at them the whole time. Even more unbelievably, it was so spicy that the heat passed through the air itself straight into their mouths, no eating required. Unbelievable, right? Tears filled everyone's eyes, making it impossible to see—even the android was affected. Iona had insisted that they weren't tears, but simply "a fluid wash for her eyes."

After that, they'd collected a long series of spices. Blade had no idea what they were all for. Well, he had a general hunch—this was the king being selfish again; he probably wanted to use these ingredients to create some kind of "ultimate meal."

Blade was of a mind to complain, but everyone else was holding it in, completing their "practical training" which was basically a glorified shopping trip. So he swallowed his gripes and continued the grueling hunt.

Besides, Earnest would give him a massage in the bath once they got back. And she wasn't the only one doing them anymore, either. Now a bunch of the girls were taking turns.

o Scene XI: The Carrot

"Well, *this* one's sure quiet."

According to the catalog, that day's ingredient was a simple carrot.

They could see green leaves sprouting up above the surface; the main body was down below. The ingredients so far had all screeched and growled and tried to intimidate them, so having a veggie that wasn't screaming was nice for a change.

"I don't really like carrots," said Blade.

Too bad Dione isn't here, he thought as they approached.

"Oh, you don't?" Earnest looked a bit surprised.

"Mmm? I mean, like, if they're an ingredient in something else, it's fine. I won't spit 'em out or anything."

"Oh, okay." She looked visibly relieved.

What's the deal with her?

But while this plant wasn't screeching or howling or threatening them, it was still a creature from another dimension, and so it was naturally ginormous.

"All right, hold this." Blade handed the catalog to Earnest and stepped forward.

From a distance, the plant in question looked like a carrot, but up close, it was more like a tree. Blade figured the vegetable buried in the ground was at least as big as a person.

"Oof…"

He grabbed the green leaves and tried a couple of practice pulls. The resistance seemed minimal—he liked his chances.

"Oh, wait! Blade, hold on! Once you pull it out…!" Earnest, list in hand, was shouting and trying to stop him.

"Huh?"

But she was a little too late. The orange part of the carrot had just breached the soil.

Hraaaaaaaaaaaaaaaaaaaaaaaaaaaaaaaaaaaaaaaaaaaah…!!

Blade heard a tremendous scream. Then he took a direct hit from point-blank range and felt his consciousness begin to fade.

✳

While Blade wasn't fully knocked out, it still took him several minutes to start moving again.

"H-hey... You all right, guys?"

He crawled back to the other students. Despite everyone else being several yards farther away, they had all been knocked down, too. Half of them were sprawled out on the ground; the other half had fully passed out. Even Earnest and Sophie appeared to have taken a lot of psychic damage.

"...What was that?" Blade asked. "A psychic attack?"

He recalled Earnest trying to stop him earlier.

"On the back of the datasheet," she said, "there was a tiny footnote. It said the carrot would scream if you pulled it out...and anyone who heard it would die..."

Aha. So that's what it was.

Blade had only pulled it part of the way out. That must have saved them from the more dire consequences. If he had lifted it all the way and they were exposed to the entire unmuffled scream, even he, an ex-Hero, might have been toast.

His head was still spinning.

"You have to read these things more carefully, all right?" Earnest scolded.

"Okay, I will. I'll read the whole thing."

Shouldn't the king have led with the dying part, though?!

"Ummm..." Earnest rubbed her temples and began reading again. "This one is called the greater mandrake. It's an evolved form of mandrake that can grow up to three and a half feet in length. The regular-sized mandrakes up on the surface are derived from this species. The part buried in the ground is a rare sort of carrot shaped like a human. When pulled out, it spews lethal curses that affect any creatures nearby."

"If it kills anyone who pulls it out, how're we supposed to obtain it?"

They'd reached an impasse. They couldn't harvest the carrot. This had seemed like an easy one at first, but now they had a real conundrum on their hands.

"Blade, why don't you pull it out, and then we'll revive you if you die?" Earnest tried her best to make this sound like a brilliant idea.

"Forget it."

"I was just joking."

"How am I supposed to know that?"

"I...," Sophie began, but Blade stopped her before she could say anything else.

She could tap into her artificial Hero force for ten seconds, letting her bend the rules of physics. Maybe then she could pull up the carrot without taking any damage... But apart from a few people, Sophie's power was still being kept secret from most of the school. She *had* used it in a pinch on several occasions, but no one else had witnessed it firsthand. It didn't seem like anyone suspected that Sophie's hidden power was that of a Hero, but Blade still felt there was no reason to let the cat out of the bag just for a little gardening work.

"Guess I'll do it, then," he said.

He'd thought of a few ideas already. They could tie a rope to the carrot and try to haul it out from a safe distance. Or they could bring in an animal and have it do the job for them, in effect sacrificing it. Or, if it was really a curse, Blade might be able to use a special kind of spirit kneading to deal with it.

"Step away, please." But then Iona pushed the crowd aside and stepped forward. "All of you seem to have forgotten that I am not a human being. Lethal curses that apply only to living creatures do not work on me."

She was being smug about it, of course. She wasted no time grabbing the leaves of the greater mandrake.

"Whoa, whoa, whoa, whoa! Wait, wait, wait, wait!"

The group physically restrained her, then shuffled back from the plant as fast as they could. The intensity of that scream had been seared directly into their minds.

They all moved away, dragging along the unlucky few who hadn't woken up yet. Once everyone was a safe distance away, they gave the signal to Iona...and she plucked out the carrot, just like that.

There was the terrifying *Hraaaaaaaaaaaahhhhh!!* again. The sound pierced through their brains even with their ears covered.

A dark spiral began to wrap itself around Iona's body. The curse had materialized as a black pattern in the air, circling her. But—perhaps because possessing her was impossible—it wound up dissipating in seconds.

"I observed an unusual aggregate of data just now. However, due to protocol incompatibilities, no interaction occurred between us. It is safe now."

A gigantic crimson carrot shaped like a person dangled from her hand. It had a face, too, its mouth wide open like it was still in its death throes.

"Um…" Earnest's face twitched. "Well, it's supposed to taste really good. We'll just cut it up into little pieces, and it should be fine."

Cool, thought Blade. *Though it'll be the king, not me, who's eating it.*

○ Scene XII: The Last Supper

The night before they retrieved the last item on the list, they held something of a dinner party at camp. Madam had whipped up a feast for everyone, but the students didn't seem all that excited.

"Ahh, you have truly amazed me! All of you have made such remarkable progress!"

The king was in a great mood, and everyone knew what that meant.

As usual, he was surrounded by beautiful women serving him the finest drinks and snacks. He kept interrupting his speech to say things like "Okay, stick it in my mouth, *ahhhh*" and "yummy, yummy," which did nothing to improve morale.

The ingredients they'd worked so hard to gather were, for some reason, nowhere on his plate. The king's meal was prepared using only ingredients brought down from the surface. *So when's he gonna eat it?* Not that Blade really cared.

"Now! Thanks to the rather excessive amount of hunting you've done, the ecosystem of the Royal Larder has been transformed! In fact, during the next few years, the overall wildlife population in this space is expected to drop precipitously, dozens of times over!"

…Is that good? Or did we just trigger a mass extinction event?

A lot of the students seemed confused. Many stopped nibbling on the cartoonishly gigantic slabs of meat in their hands and began staring at them in silence. From their faces, it seemed they'd just awakened to a sobering truth—their voracious appetites were destroying the environment.

"Ha-ha-ha! Don't worry. If we could hunt this place to extinction, we would have done it a long time ago! The wildlife here are all like weeds in a garden. You pull them and pull them, and yet they always come back."

I bet you haven't done any weeding in your life. And we did all the work this time, too!

But his semi-plausible explanation and self-satisfied look were good enough for everyone else. As always, the king's skill at oratory was top-class. He'd deceived Blade a lot, too, back during his Hero days.

"Now, eat up! Have as much as you want, for a good meal today will be your energy for tomorrow! And tomorrow will be the last one! The moment of truth!"

At the king's signal, everyone let loose their ravenous appetites.

○ Scene XIII: The King

"The moment of truth" was right. There, on the final page of the catalog, were the words *The King*—and nothing else. (There was an addendum specifying that he was "strong and tasty," but that wasn't much help. In this dimension, strength and flavor went hand in hand. If something was the strongest, it was naturally also the most delicious.)

"Do we *really* need this guy's meat for the main dish?" Blade asked.

There, at the base of a huge tree that pierced both the sky above and the earth below, sat a gigantic monster—a combination of a bull and a man. It had the head and lower body of a bull, but it stood upright on two legs. In its hands, it held a massive war hammer, easily thirty feet in length, providing a handy yardstick for estimating the height of the creature wielding it.

It had probably already noticed them. The students could feel a seemingly infinite number of eyes upon them. The creature's breath, visibly white in the morning air, was filled with bloodlust.

"Um... Main dish?'" a distressed-looking Earnest asked. "Blade... Did you already figure it out...?"

"Well, of course I did."

"Oh, way to go, Earnest," Ovie said, braids untied and fully prepared for battle. "You said you were using your 'natural charm spell' to fool him, too."

"I… I did exactly as Yessica instructed!"

What exactly was a "natural charm spell"? Did she mean all that cheek and breast touching in the bath, and how she kept tracing her finger down his back?

"What were you hiding from me?" Blade asked.

"Huh? Didn't you just say you'd figured it out?"

"Well, yeah. The king's having us gather ingredients so he can cook up and eat the ultimate meal, the one thing he wants to eat the most. Anyone woulda noticed that." *Who the heck was too dense to figure that one out?* "So, what were you hiding from me?"

"Oh, it's fine. Don't worry about it… Let's just focus on the enemy right now. Okay?"

Earnest latched on to Blade's back and pressed *them* against it—her breasts, of course. *Yep, this must be what she meant by "natural charm spell."*

Blade concentrated on his opponent, just as she'd instructed. The "king" was still sitting at the base of the overly tall tree, staring at them.

"This tree is called the Main Shaft. It is where the density of nourishment leaking from the engine is at its highest. The area is occupied by the strongest creatures in the Larder."

Iona was carrying on as Eliza nodded along. No one else seemed to understand, however, so Blade assumed he didn't need to follow.

"It's moving," said Earnest.

Blade faced forward. The bull-headed monster at the base of the tree—or the "Main Shaft"?—had risen up. He must have gotten tired of watching Blade and the others hiding in the bushes.

Right. Let's do this.

○ Scene XIV: The Start of the Battle

The 108 students fanned out and then began to close the distance. They proceeded at an excruciatingly slow pace, just a few inches at a time, to ensure no platoon was separated from the battalion.

Around the massive tree called the Main Shaft was a vast expense of barren land. Not even grass grew on it, because the level of nourishment was beyond what normal creatures could process. The view from the tree eliminated the possibility of a surprise attack. If they wanted to engage this foe, they had to get closer first.

The bull-headed monster, still holding his big war hammer, watched them and roared loudly from time to time. He was easily over thirty feet tall, and the hammer was sized to fit him, making it less a hand-to-hand weapon and more like a tool for attacking a castle. It seemed absurd to use it against a single person.

Everyone was thinking the same thing—that this was impossible. Getting hit with a weapon like that—the size of a building—would flatten anyone. All the training in the world wouldn't save them.

Well, it's pretty surprising what people can do if they train a whole lot. They really can achieve anything. It seemed that only Blade was thinking optimistically, however.

The rest of their thoughts were more along the line of: *Oh man, oh man, we're toast.*

Blade didn't think they were that bad off in terms of strength. In terms of enthusiasm, however, they were losing big time. The creature before them was indeed a "king"—on a whole different level from the other ingredients.

The bull-headed monster hefted its giant war hammer above its head and let out an animalistic roar. Everyone involuntarily reared back, wiping out the last three minutes' progress.

We are toast, toast, toast!

Blade really did think they had a chance, at least in terms of fighting power. Since coming to this world, they had been engaged in actual battle every day while hunting. Everyone had been polishing their skills, as well as eating incredibly nutritious food, thus boosting their physical strength. Their life force, the key ingredient in spirit and magic, was only increasing. This was "dragon-style" training. Dragons didn't train, of course—they powered themselves up by consuming.

Basically, everyone was stronger now, but the process had been so rapid that they couldn't see their own improvement. That, and spending every day hunting had softened them up mentally. In effect, they had forgotten how to fight against someone clearly stronger than them.

Blade, of course, had trouble understanding this. As a Hero, he had battled against stronger foes every day. An easy fight, where he was just bullying a weak opponent, was almost unheard of. Every battle had been impossible, reckless, ridiculous; but it was up to the Hero to win anyway. Back when he was serving the king, he was always being sent to places with big bosses beyond his level.

Fwrrrrsh.

The bull-headed monster exhaled. Its breath was so hot it was no different from steam. *Yeah. I always fought big bosses just like this guy.*

"Ha-ha-ha! Look at that, Sirene! Looking good, no? Seems like they're in quite a predicament!"

At least that drunk old man was enjoying this. The king was hanging out at a safe distance having a wild party—girls, booze, food, you name it. Pure debauchery.

"What every good youth needs is a challenge! Obstacles in their way! And once they overcome them, there will be victory, glory, women, and fine wine!"

"He—um, I mean, Blade! Hang in there!" Dione was cheering for them, but that was it.

The "reserve force" drinking in the rear consisted of twelve former champions, current generals, and semi-champions that all served the king. About six champions in all—a "champion" here being a unit of combat power. The students kept glancing back at them, wondering why the adults were refusing to help.

Ugh. Great. That is absolutely terrible for morale, you know.

It wasn't like the students were pushovers. They had worked to create the best possible platoons of six soldiers each, dividing up tanks, attackers, and offensive magic casters—even considering things like individual compatibility and romantic relationships. At their current skill level, a platoon like this would qualify as a semi-champion, and three six-person platoons had the same force as a full champion. A company of eighteen students, then, would count as a champion.

Thinking about it like that, they were a pretty impressive force. With 108 students, they had six eighteen-person companies—in other words, six champions. What's more, five of the students—Earnest, Sophie, Ovie, Iona, and Cú—were comparable to semi-champions all by themselves, almost two champions worth of fighting power. Ein and Zwei, flying overhead, were immature, but they were still much stronger than your typical magic beast. They, too, could count as semi-champions. And then there was Blade. At 15 percent, he might qualify as a champion, but it was a little iffy.

In total, their force rated at around nine champions.

See? All those drunken idiots in the rear are nothing more than reserves.

Blade glanced over at Earnest. As expected, she refused to be outdone in terms of drive. Nothing could break her spirit. After all, her role was to spur people on and inspire them to do their best.

"What's up? Aren't you gonna say something?" he asked.

She stared back at him blankly.

Look at your friends, he wanted to tell her. *They're losing before the battle has even begun.*

Instead, he took a step forward.

"All right, guys!" he called out. "Let's do this!"

But just as he readied his sword, preparing to deal the first blow to the "king"...the beast was battered by a huge blow from the side.

Chomp!

They heard a strange sound, almost comical. It seemed to demand their full attention, erasing everything else.

Graaaaaaaaaaarrrrh!!

A giant beast howled in rage. The bull-headed monster from a moment ago was...still there, but only the bottom half of it. Standing atop its remains was another gigantic beast, this one on four legs. It was even more bold and fearless than the last one, and far more enormous. Opening its mouth wide, it took another bite. Now only the ankles remained from the bull-headed menace.

"Huh? Um…"

Blade and his companions were left in the dust.

Um…what exactly happened just now…?

"Whoa! Look at that!" exclaimed the old man. "We have a new king in our midst! What could he be think-*king*?!"

"Oh, very droll of you, Gil. Let me fill up your glass."

"Hya-ha-ha!"

The king hugged the beautiful women to his left and right and laughed like a dirty old man. Sirene, who was pouring the wine, was also slightly intoxicated. You'd *have* to be drunk to laugh at a joke that stupid.

"A slab of beef would've been great…but I hear behemoth meat is delicious, too! All right, all of you—happy hunting! The former king is dead, but that just means you'll have to take down his replacement!"

The old man was in incredibly high spirits, and the drinking was in full swing.

So this weird creature is a behemoth?

It was a four-legged beast with well-developed muscles and a pair of huge horns protruding from both sides of its body. Surely, it must be a survivor from the Age of Divinity. Its huge figure was covered with tough, armor-like skin, and drool like boiling water was dripping from its impressive jaws, melting into the ground below.

"Umm…?"

Blade thought for a bit, trying his best to grasp the situation.

The "king" was now out of the picture. Another creature had usurped the throne by gobbling him up headfirst, and now the bull-headed monster that had seemed so strong was packed away in the newcomer's stomach.

At that point, Blade realized something very distressing. If this monster had defeated the last "king" with a single bite, it had to be *way* stronger.

Oh, man. What now?

"Stop looking scared, Blade," said Earnest.

"Huh? What? Who, me? …*Me*?!" Blade pointed to himself.

Me?! *I was just trying to think of what to do since everyone* else *is scared.*

"Oh. I see. So you thought everyone else was scared."

"What?" Blade stared back at Earnest.

"It's all right, Blade."

"What?" Now he turned toward Sophie.

"I was just a little tired, is all."

"What?"

Ovie was yawning, tears forming in the corners of her eyes.

"This one looks a lot tastier!" said Cú.

"What? Huh?"

"You see? And that goes for the rest of you, right?" The academy's Empress addressed her 107 fellow students. "Don't you think it would be anticlimactic if that bull guy was our final opponent?"

Everyone nodded—all 107 of them. Or to be exact, 107 plus one plus one.

Screee, screee...

Ein and Zwei were calling out from above. Now it was 107 plus one plus one plus *two* nods.

"Ha-ha-ha! What a dependable bunch!" The king stood up and applauded. "And our Empress is truly wonderful! Now, take off your clothes!"

Earnest threw Asmodeus at him. It bounced off his face with a clang and returned to its owner's hand. By now a strong bond linked Earnest with her sword—as strong as a boomerang anyway.

Of course, once she went into Scion mode, her clothes would come off regardless of anyone's orders.

"...Do *not* look!"

All the boys were staring at Earnest's body, so she decided to give them a warning. Some turned away, thoroughly scolded, Clay and Kassim among them. Others (like Leonard) kept on staring. Nothing could make their gaze waver.

Then, without so much as a pause, Earnest turned on the gas. Still dressed, she became the Scion of Flame, burning through her animal skin loincloth and breast sash.

And with that, the battle was underway.

○ Scene XV: Clash Against the New King

The students began an all-out attack.

Earnest ran around in a circle, shooting off fireballs in rapid succession. These balls of flame, pouring down without interruption, contained several hundred thousand calories' worth of energy per shot. That was equivalent to the amount Earnest used to have back when she let herself go—that is, before she went on her diet. She had been ingesting a lot of calories in this dimension, and now she was ready to burn all of them off. Each shot was filled with enough heat to reduce any run-of-the-mill magic beast to bone.

The behemoth, however, brushed them away like flies. But even these deadly fireballs were merely meant to keep the monster in place.

"La-la-la-la-la-la-la-laaa!!"

"Hrah-hrah-hrah-hrah-hrah-hrah-hraaaah!!"

Two gales—one blue, one green—rushed up the behemoth's neck in a double helix, unleashing a barrage from both sides. Sophie and Iona, the strongest barehanded fighters in the school, had become a first-class attack duo here in the Larder. Even without any weapons, they were just as strong. And their penetrating strikes, deployed from both sides with perfectly synchronized timing, combined inside their target's body to achieve a level of force many times stronger than a single attack.

Over a dozen of these blows exploded simultaneously inside the behemoth's body. It was shaken. Not staggered, but shaken.

A torrent of fireballs from the school's deadliest flame monster was like a mosquito bite, and being hit by blow after blow from the school's best merely shook it.

"Boys! You do something, too!!"

With that scolding from the Empress, the male students sprang into action.

"Secret sword strike—*Diamond Cutter!!*"

Clay's bone sword fired off an infinite number of images of itself. It was a brilliant strike, capable of slashing through anything it touched.

"Finishing strike—*Ahh!* Look over *there!*"

Kassim pointed to the side. The behemoth followed his finger—and then, while it was distracted, he sent a dagger flying toward a gap in the beast's muscles and tendons. A poisoned dagger, of course.

Arrrrrrrrrrrgh!

It was clearly angry. *Kassim was playing dirty, after all.*

Now the behemoth began breathing flame several times more powerful than Earnest's fire. The whole group was about to be bathed in hellfire, when—

"Divine skill—*Absolute Defense!*"

—Leonard thrust his spear into the ground. The weapon let out an electrical discharge, which created a spherical barrier large enough to envelop everyone.

The move was even more powerful than it had been before. Whether it merited the descriptor "absolute" was up for debate, but it successfully held the behemoth's hellfire at bay for a few seconds.

Graaaaaaah!!

Cú, now in full dragon form, unleashed her dragon breath—the original flavor. Maybe it was all the nutrition she had taken in, but Cú's body had grown a little, and her breath packed more of a punch, too.

Flame clashed against flame. But after a few seconds of fierce competition, the behemoth's breath won out.

"*Blade? Ready yet?*" asked Earnest.

"I'm working on it!"

Not even a force equivalent to nine champions was enough to defeat this monster. In order to pull this off, they needed a skill that went beyond Blade's current 15 percent limit. If only he could use up to 30, then he'd know exactly which skill to use. But if he tapped into that much power right now, he'd surely die. So, to solve this dilemma, Blade decided to partner up with the Overlord.

"Hmm… You just keep going, don't you?" she observed.

The Overlord unleashed her full demonic power. It coursed out from her palms and into Blade's body as she pushed against him. Blade mixed this highly purified force with a small amount of his own spirit, converting it into elemental power.

Among masters of the technique, this was known as kneading—a process of drawing spirals, folding, and superimposing to transform lower-order energy into higher-order energy.

Blade proceeded to knead elemental power right up to his 15 percent limit.

"Okay, it's done! Take your hand—"

"This'll be faster," the Overlord said.

Then she grabbed the back of Blade's head—and, without another word, locked lips with him. Blade was shocked, but quickly figured out what she was doing. In another instant, he exhaled his power into the Overlord's body, as if performing artificial respiration. All that elemental power he'd just kneaded was transferred to the Overlord instantly—in the space of a single breath. Blade hadn't even known magic could be transferred that way.

The problem was the Overlord's maximum storage capacity. She had originally possessed around 30 percent of Blade's full power. That capacity was restricted now, but she should still be able to hold all the elemental power Blade had given her...

"I am about to overflow. You really filled me up..."

She gave him a bewitching smile, licked her lips, and brought one hand to her belly.

Wow, what was that? I think I just got a better understanding of the word erotic...

"*Come onnnnnnnnn! Hurry uuuuuuuuuuuuuup!!*"

Earnest was raging at them. Blade didn't know what was going on over there, but it sounded like they didn't have a lot of time.

"Right!" he said, focusing on his part of the plan.

Now he had to knead his own spirit into fighting force. He closed his eyes. His task was to finish kneading before Earnest and the others were wiped out.

"Artificial He—*koff, koff*—force! Ten seconds remaining!"

Blade heard Sophie's voice.

"Hero!" said Ovie. "Sophie just used that power of hers!"

Don't call me Hero.

"Interconnect link complete," came Iona's voice. "Transmitting power. Firing positronium particle cannon."

"Hero," Ovie said again, "That girl just fired something crazy."

I said, don't call me Hero. It's distracting!

Iona's right arm was equipped with a weapon dating from the Guardian era, one so powerful that even a Hero wouldn't want to suffer a direct hit. Now she, and Sophie, had thrown out everything they had, down to their last secret move. There was nothing left.

But Blade still wasn't done kneading his spirit.

Oh crap. Oh crap. Oh crap. I've done it now!

But Blade didn't panic. After all—

"After all, he's the He— *Mmph!* Hey, let go!"

"The king's howling nonsense," said Ovie.

Blade didn't need her to tell him that. The king was always like this. And he was wrong, too.

Blade didn't panic because he trusted the others would pull through.

"Guys! Hang in there! Blade'll work it out! Trust him!"

And they believed in him, too. That was why he could do the same.

Okay. All done.

Blade opened his eyes wide. He shouted to Earnest as the fighting force coursing through his body sent sparks this way and that.

"Earnest! Your sword!"

"About time!"

She hurled the magic sword Asmodeus toward Blade. It spun through the air and landed in his hand.

"Okay, Asmodeus, do it."

"Wait—" shouted Asmodeus.

No. No waiting. The behemoth, too much for even nine champions to handle, was a spirit beast. This was the only way to slice one up. He needed a move capable of fighting both holy and demonic forces—*Holy Demon Blade!*

"Stop! Stop, stop! That skill! I can't! No! No! Nooooooo!!"

"Hang in there."

"Nooooo!! I—I caaaaaaan't!"

Asmodeus was being held by two hands—one Blade's, one the Overlord's. From their two arms, two kinds of energy—fighting force and elemental power—poured in. Blade couldn't use this technique by himself anymore. But if he charged up the Overlord with his elemental power and they each contributed 15 percent, they could team up to reach the 30 percent necessary.

The sword, wrapped in blue and red spirals running in opposite directions, shone with a radiance that transcended both the holy and demonic.

"Let's go, Overlord."

"As much as you like!"

The two of them swung the blade down.

"Whoooooooaaaaaa!!"

"Yaaaaaaaaaaaaaaaaaah!!"

A giant arc of pure light shot out, smashing into the behemoth headfirst. Its natural barrier blocked the initial hit, but the force of their strike shattered first one layer, then two, then three, four, five, and six.

"Mmm," said Ovie, "that's what got *me*, too."

"It's over," Blade announced as the last barrier broke.

First, a vertical line appeared on the behemoth's face. Then its body began to dislocate along that line. Its left and right sides each fell in a different direction, opening up its body like a yawning mouth. The two halves, their surfaces as smooth as a mirror's, fell away into two even chunks of meat.

Once he'd watched all of this transpire, Blade fell to the ground.

"Hmm? Are you dying, Hero?" asked Ovie.

"Not dying. Just tired." Blade was only able to speak because he'd successfully kept his power output under 15 percent, allowing him to survive. "Also…I am *so* hungry."

"Mmm. Well, you won't have to wait long."

He could hear the Overlord saying something and feel someone lifting up his head and placing it somewhere soft.

He was resting on the Overlord's lap.

As shouts of joy echoed in the distance, Blade's consciousness drifted away.

○ Scene: Epilogue

"Okay. All set."

The doctor pulled off one examination glove, then the other, and tossed them into the trash. Blade pulled up his pants, tears in his eyes.

"Why are you crying?" she asked.

"You wouldn't understand!"

After returning to the surface with everyone else, Blade had gone back to the doctor's office for a routine checkup. This was his first full medical exam in some time. He thought he'd gotten pretty reckless toward the end of his stay in the Royal Larder, after all. He didn't really mind his power limit decreasing. In fact, he welcomed it. It brought him that much closer to being a normal person. But if he *didn't* know his limit, he might accidentally go over it and die.

"So how's it look?" he asked.

"Well…not bad. Not bad at all."

The doctor took a minute to think as she tapped Blade's patient chart with the back of her finger. Blade couldn't help noticing the implication in her gesture.

"Just give me the results."

"Since your last exam, you're three percent—"

"Lower?!"

"No, higher. You should be okay to use up to eighteen percent now."

"Huh?" Blade blinked. Higher? It wasn't going down?

"Wait, what? Why?"

"Well, you're eating sensibly, engaging in moderate exercise, taking care of yourself… I suppose it's all paying off."

Come to think of it, over in the Larder, all he'd done was eat and sleep, really. He'd been living a terribly simple life. Did all that hunting count as "moderate exercise"? Would Earnest's massages count as "taking care of himself"?

"Like I always tell you," she said. "what you need most of all is rest."

Blade resented how the doctor always spoke to him like she was the older one. She was, but that wasn't the point.

"Well, I don't really know *how* to rest. I've never done it before."

If a Hero rested, it'd be the end of the world.

"But that's what you're doing right now. Resting."

"Oh, I guess so." Blade nodded meekly.

"By the way," she continued, scribbling on his chart, "have you had lunch yet?"

"Oh, um, no."

He was zoning out, staring at the nape of her neck, when he suddenly jumped up.

"Oh, right! It's lunchtime!"

He was just turning to leave when she said, "Well, I hope you're ready for a treat," winking at the door as it closed behind him.

What was she talking about? he wondered.

Blade hurried to the dorm's dining hall. Lunch break was almost over, and he was worried they might have already packed up the buffet. But for some reason, everybody was still there—108 people, one dragon, and one android. All of them.

"Happy birthday, Blade!"

A couple of party crackers went off.

"Happy...birthday? Huh? What?"

Blade stood there, dazed, paper streamers dangling from his face. Earnest walked up to him, smiling. She wore a conical hat on her head.

"Today's your birthday."

"My birthday?"

"Blade, if someone's birthday is unknown, it's customary to celebrate it on the day they were found," Sophie said, utterly serious.

She was wearing a pair of dark glasses with a fake mustache attached to them, and the mismatch was driving him crazy.

"Huh? Wuh? Buh?"

"And my honored Father was found exactly seventeen years ago today. I made my own birthday the day my honored Father tamed me, so we'll have *my* birthday next year, too. But today we're celebrating *you*!"

At Cú's words, Blade looked up. The whole dining hall had been decorated. Festive paper chains were hanging everywhere, and flowers, paper spheres, and stars were all over the place. He had stopped by before going to the infirmary, and everything had been normal then. In so little time, it had changed completely. Now it was all decked out like the farewell party they'd thrown for Iona.

"Master, human beings celebrate both their birth and their termination."

"Huh? What? …This is a celebration? You're celebrating me? Really? *Me?*"

He didn't get it. At all. Who would celebrate a Hero?

A Hero was meant to fight and fight and fight, all to keep everyone else smiling.

Huh? What?

"Now you're the same age as me," Earnest said. Come to think of it, she was right.

"You're *older* than me?"

"I sure am. You should be more respectful."

"You see?" Yessica cut in. "It's just like I said. Blade's never had anyone celebrate his birthday."

She was right, of course.

"We all planned this," Claire said, looking up at Blade. "We talked about what to give you as a present, but we weren't sure…"

"So," continued Earnest, closing in on him, "I asked you. And you answered, didn't you?"

"Huh? What? Me? What did I say?"

"Don't you remember? I asked what you wanted for your birthday, and you said 'katsu curry'… Oh, was I wrong? What? Oh, no, did I mess this up?"

Blade vaguely recalled their conversation. A *looooong* time ago, before this mess with the Larder, everyone had been talking about birthdays. Blade had gotten all sulky because he couldn't participate, and then Earnest had asked him what he'd like as a birthday present, and he'd said, "Katsu curry"...

"Ahhh! I *did* say that! I did! I really did!"

"I knew it! *Whew!* Thank goodness."

Earnest sighed in relief. Then she looked back up, regained her composure, and shouted toward the back of the dining hall.

"All right! So Blade's birthday present...is right here! Dun, dun, *dunnn!* Madam, go ahead!"

The dining hall lady brought in a huge plate that required two hands to carry. On it was what looked like enough food for ten people...

"Everything here's from the Royal Larder! The ultimate in gourmet cuisine, crafted from one hundred percent pure ingredients! The ultimate katsu curry!"

"The curry spice is from the Killer-Smile Peppers—remember that grin? The veggies are Land Mine Potatoes and Greater Mandrakes...and make sure you eat all those carrots, too!"

A salad was also brought in.

"The salad is made of shredded Emperor Cabbage and punched up with Vampire Tomatoes and Gatling Green Peas. Lovely, isn't it? And it's topped with the Boxing Corn, that sweet, sweet corn you spent fifteen rounds fighting."

"To coat the meat," said Madam, "I baked some bread with that killer yeast, then made bread crumbs out of it. I fried it all in oil from those sunflowers, of course."

"And the coup de grace, the meat itself...!" Earnest lifted a finger to the heavens, then slashed it down in a swordlike motion. "The 'king' of the Royal Larder! The flesh from the spirit beast behemoth!"

On the very top of the giant plate of curry was a cut of fried meat as big as Dione's butt. It was covered in golden bread crumbs and looked absolutely delicious.

"Phew! Boy, we sure had a tough time down there, huh?" said Earnest.

Everyone solemnly nodded.

It wasn't exactly easy for me, either. Especially that Boxing Corn...

"Ha-ha-ha! I couldn't help overhearing you!" The king appeared with a hearty laugh.

"Since when were you here, Your Majesty?" Earnest audibly clicked her tongue.

"I showed up around the time you said 'Now you're the same age as me! ♡'!"

"For the record, I didn't add a ♡... Well," she continued, managing to sound both courteous and condescending as she addressed the king, "I suppose His Majesty helped out by providing a location for this round of 'practical training.'"

Blade wasn't really listening. He was just sitting in his chair, staring at the katsu curry in front of him. It began to look a bit weird—distorted, like it was staring to warp.

"By the way, Blade, what are you doing?" asked the king.

"W-well... I... I'm just not used to...this kind of thing... I don't know how it works, so..."

Blade had been working hard to keep back his tears. Someone had once told him that boys weren't supposed to cry.

"Come on, you fool! This is *exactly* when a man should cry! By my name as Gilgamesh Soulmaker, I hereby approve your reaction! And I take back anything I said in the past about men and not crying! ...Yes, cry all you want, lad!"

Blade took up his spoon...and began furiously eating. He ate and ate. He ate all that curry as tears streamed down his face. He ate the behemoth meat as snot dripped from his nose.

Thank you, behemoth. I mean it. You're soooo delicious. And...thanks, everyone. For the first time, I feel like l was really born into this world.

Afterword

Well, I now have all four colors of the Windows flag together. It turned into a pale blue two-tone with Windows 10, but let's forget about that. What am I talking about? The characters' colors, of course.

From the original planning stages, the characters of *Classroom for Heroes* were referred to by their colors. Earnest was the "red heroine," Sophie the "blue heroine," Cú the "yellow heroine," and so on—those were the code names we used. When the "image colors" of each character are well-balanced, it helps accentuate each cast member's charms—or that's what I, Araki, believe anyway.

When red, blue, and yellow are lined up together, the results are fetching and catch the eye. Each color helps to bring out the best in the others. When the easily riled Earnest is put together with the chill Sophie, it helps break out and emphasize both of their personalities. Add the yellow, boisterous Cú, and the green, easy-going Iona, and everything only gets better, much like the four colors in the Windows flag.

We'll continue assigning image colors to each character going forward in *Classroom for Heroes*. If we ever have a chance to hold a public celebration or something for this series, be sure to bring the right glowstick color for your favorite character.

Incidentally, after three volumes, *Classroom for Heroes* has been getting some very good reviews. As the author, it's a big load off my mind. I promise I'm not wearing a smug smile over here, though. I've put on a stern frown, like a mountain ascetic.

For now, I'm producing volumes on a four-month cycle. Volume 4 should hit stores in early 2016, and there's a chance it'll have a different vibe from the first three. Maybe. Each volume so far has consisted of three chapters, but the next one will have a section jam-packed with various short stories followed by a Sophie-centric episode.

Also, on September 18, 2016—a week before Volume 3 comes out— *Classroom for Heroes: Empress of Flame* will go on sale in Japan. This is a manga adaptation by Takashi Minakuchi, and the first chapter will tell Earnest's story from her perspective, so I think it'll offer something refreshingly different from the novels.

Changing the subject a little, the light novel industry is being taken over by a wave of webnovels lately.

There's a website called *Shousetsuka ni Narou*, or "Let's Become a Novelist," and a lot of the series posted on there are receiving traditional publications and turning into big hits. I, too, have some novel series running on that site—*C-Mart Prospering in Another World*, and one more as of August 2015. *Stardust Hero Chronicles*, one of my more popular early works, is already being published by Dengeki Bunko/Pony Canyon Books in Japan, and another book launch is in the works. *C-Mart*, too, is slated to get published under the Dash X Bunko label, so be on the lookout for that one as well.

Finally, here are some QR codes for my webnovels and the *Classroom for Heroes* feedback form. Please note that all the websites linked are available in Japanese only.

Classroom for Heroes Volume 3 feedback

http://www.araki-shin.com/araki/eiyu3.htm

C-Mart Prospering in Another World series page

http://ncode.syosetu.com/n6170cq/

Stardust Hero Chronicles series page

http://ncode.syosetu.com/n5976cr/

About the author

Shin Araki

A character-oriented novelist who's doing all kinds of work in the light novel industry. Taking a summer break this July to rest and refresh. Member #001 of the More Win-Win Slow-Life Light Novels Society.

Illustrator: Haruyuki Morisawa

A Tokyo-based illustrator from Toyama Prefecture. I had hernia surgery, and I'm feeling a lot lighter now!

HAVE YOU BEEN TURNED ON TO LIGHT NOVELS YET?

86—EIGHTY-SIX, VOL. 1-12

In truth, there is no such thing as a bloodless war. Beyond the fortified walls protecting the eighty-five Republic Sectors lies the "nonexistent" Eighty-Sixth Sector. The young men and women of this forsaken land are branded the Eighty-Six and, stripped of their humanity, pilot "unmanned" weapons into battle...

Manga adaptation available now!

WOLF & PARCHMENT, VOL. 1-9

The young man Col dreams of one day joining the holy clergy and departs on a journey from the bathhouse, Spice and Wolf. Winfiel Kingdom's prince has invited him to help correct the sins of the Church. But as his travels begin, Col discovers in his luggage a young girl with a wolf's ears and tail named Myuri, who stowed away for the ride!

Manga adaptation available now!

SOLO LEVELING, VOL. 1-8

E-rank hunter Jinwoo Sung has no money, no talent, and no prospects to speak of—and apparently, no luck, either! When he enters a hidden double dungeon one fateful day, he's abandoned by his party and left to die at the hands of some of the most horrific monsters he's ever encountered.

Comic adaptation available now!